THE CAROLINA CAPER

AN ADVENTURE GUILD STORY

ERNEST DEMPSEY

CHANDLER DEMPSEY

138 PUBLISHING

PROLOGUE

NORTH CAROLINA-1937

The rickety old car rumbled down the gravel road, kicking up clouds of dust that churned and seemed to hang a little before slowly billowing, then dissolving, into the humid summer air.

Louis Hammond had been driving for a while and was thankful for the temporary shade the passing trees provided along the side of the road. Where he was from, in California, the oppressive Southern heat and humidity existed only in rumors and lore. Now, he was getting a chance to experience it firsthand. It was real.

His button-up shirt was soaked in sweat, and his forehead leaked streams of perspiration down his nose and chubby cheeks. His fingers and palms were clammy with a mix of his own sweat and the boiling humidity as he reached for his handkerchief for the millionth time that day to dab his forehead and face dry.

Still, all things considered, it had been a good trip.

He'd decided to take a vacation and drive around the Eastern Seaboard, cruising along through the forests and farmlands of North Carolina on this particular week. Aside from the omnipresent heat, he found it to be a delightful drive. The hills and mountains were covered in thick, lush trees that displayed green in every shade. Fields of golden-and-green grass and sunflowers whizzed by occasionally, as well as seemingly endless fields of tobacco, corn, pumpkins, and sweet potatoes.

Everywhere he looked, he saw signs of the slow, relaxed way of the South, a dramatic contrast to some of the big cities he frequented.

It had been a wonderful vacation, and he felt a pang in his chest at the thought of returning home, not that where he lived was so bad. If he hated it so much, he'd have left long ago. Still, he felt as though there were something calling him here, to this place that was so quiet, so peaceful, so abundant and green.

He knew, of course, that it wasn't always so. Winters here weren't as harsh as they were in the North, but they still hit hard, and many parts of North Carolina could be dunked in frigid temperatures and even the occasional dousing of snow.

He was happy to skip dealing with winter. Where he lived, it was nothing more than an urban legend, regaled by far-off peoples from a mythical land. Well, except in the mountains in California. They sometimes got snow as late as May.

He dismissed the thought as he felt his stomach grumble for what must have been the hundredth time in the last hour. He pressed his lips together and clenched his jaw, feeling the hunger pangs pulse through his abdomen and signal his brain that it was way past time to eat. His forehead wrinkled as he thought for a moment. There were no places to eat around here, not that he knew of. He was still out in the country and possibly another half hour away from a town where he could get a bite. The map on the passenger seat wouldn't be much help, but he'd been trying not to look at it too often, instead choosing to let himself get "lost" in the journey. He'd eventually find civilization again. Probably sooner rather than later.

When his stomach growled again, though, he licked his lips and noticed rows of hickory trees passing by along the side of the road. Where there were hickory trees, there were nuts.

Unwilling to postpone eating for the indeterminate future, Hammond pulled off onto the shoulder of the road and stopped the car. He climbed out, dabbing his forehead again with his rag that was nearly as soaked as his shirt. He took a deep breath, looked around for a moment, and noticed a particularly large hickory standing on the other side of the road, just beyond the shallow ditch that ran along the edge of the packed gravel road.

Without the rumble of the engine and the squeaking of the springs under his seat, the world around him fell into a peaceful silence, only interrupted by the songs of birds in the canopy above and the chirps of chipmunks and squirrels.

"Sure is nice here," he said, momentarily forgetting the over-whelming heat and his revolting stomach.

After looking both ways, he crossed the road. It was an act of habit, checking to make sure no cars were coming. Were there any on the road, he would have heard them from a mile away.

Hammond reached the ditch on the other side and looked down the length of it in both directions. He stepped down into the barren ditch and then up the other side, careful not to slip on the grass. He straightened his back and realized it had been a while since he stretched, so he put his hands over his head and reached his fingers to the sky until he felt his spine click a few times. Then Hammond tilted to the right and left, shaking out the opposing leg as he leaned one way then the other.

"That's better," he said.

Already feeling rejuvenated, Hammond began searching the ground near an old fence that ran the length of an overgrown field. There were hickory nuts scattered around on the dirt and grass, along with a few other kinds of nuts from the various trees that accompa-nied the hickories, including a stray pinecone or two.

Hammond bent down and meticulously picked up one nut after the other until he'd collected two handfuls. Then he stuffed them into his pockets, snagged a few more, and made his way back across the road. A large rock jutted out of the ground about fifteen feet away from his car, and he decided that was as good a place as any to consume his foraged fare.

After dusting off the rock to clear it of any loose debris and dirt, he sat down and emptied his pockets of the nuts. Using a little ingenuity, Hammond picked up a smaller rock, placed a nut on a slight cradle of the boulder he was using as a seat, and hit the nut on the side.

He was pleased to see it crack relatively easily, revealing the meat within. He scooped up the contents, popped them into his mouth, and grabbed another of the nuts to repeat the process.

Hammond ate like this for several minutes, taking the time to the simple meal in this quiet place. He felt like he was on an expedition, roughing it like pioneers might have done a hundred years before, although they would have been on horseback or wagons—the less fortunate on foot.

He finished the last of the nuts and savored the earthy flavor then stood up, dusted his pants of a few shards of nutshells, and started to head back to the car. He glanced back to make sure he hadn't dropped anything important when he noticed something strange sticking up out of the ground near the boulder.

It was a smaller stone, flatter than the rock he'd used to crack nuts —and also larger. He cocked his head to the side, inspecting the anomaly as his feet unconsciously carried him toward the object. As he drew closer, he could see that most of the rock was exposed, leaving only one end of it partially covered by leaves, dirt, and grass. When he reached the stone, he bent down at the waist to get a closer look.

Immediately, Hammond stiffened. He stood erect, his head swiveling back and forth rapidly to make sure there was no one else around. A chill shot through his body, reflected by the goosebumps on his arms and neck.

The stone had writing engraved on it.

In its position, not far from the boulder he'd been sitting on a moment before, it was about twenty to thirty feet off of the road. It would have been easy to miss by anyone passing by or even by workers who'd completed the road construction here. Unless they'd chosen to use the boulder as a table and seat, as he'd done, the stone would have gone unnoticed for years, maybe decades.

He took one last wary glance in both directions and then crouched down on one knee.

Hammond reached out his right hand and pinched the exposed edge of the rock between his index finger and thumb. He gave the object a tug but found it to be stubbornly stuck in the earth. Using both hands, he wiggled the stone until it broke free of the natural bonds.

The man let out a sigh as if the exercise had exhausted him.

He wiped his fingers across the surface of the slightly curved stone and locked his gaze on the inscription. It was writing unlike anything he'd ever seen before. Some of the words were similar to English but spelled in a way that was completely foreign. There was an unmistakable symbol also carved into the flat surface of the top. It was a cross. His eyes flitted to four numbers at the bottom. His eyelids gaped open as he read the numbers out loud.

"Fifteen ninety-one?"

It was hard to read due to the weathering that the stone had endured for...centuries, apparently. *But that couldn't be right, could it*, Louis wondered. *The year 1591? Is that when this was carved?*

"That's impossible," he muttered.

In his mind, he started calculating dates he recalled from history classes. "Columbus sailed the ocean in 1492," he said. "But 1591...that was still early in colonial history."

A crow cawed from somewhere in the trees above, the sound startling the man from his deep thought. He nearly fell over backward from the sudden noise and realized his legs were starting to lose circulation as the backs of his knees started to itch. He stood up straight again and examined the stone more closely.

It was difficult to read, both due to the language that it was written in and the effects of time and deterioration. He sighed, glancing down the road in both directions again, just to make sure no one saw him. He felt like a thief, taking this stone from its resting place, though he doubted it belonged to anyone. If it did, they wouldn't have left it there.

He needed to know what it was, who had written on it, and who left it there. He had a friend at Emory University in Atlanta who might be able to lend a hand with deciphering what exactly this rock was and who put it in the dirt next to the road.

He snorted at the last thought. If someone placed the object there, he doubted there would have been a semblance of a road. Perhaps it had been an animal path or a trail for horses and people on foot, but there would have been no road in 1591—that is, if the stone was indeed legitimate.

Hammond could feel his heart pounding in his chest as he carried the rock back to his car and laid it down in the back. Then he changed his mind, not wanting to let the thing out of his sight. He picked it up and set it down on the passenger side of the front seat then started the rattling engine.

Before he shifted the vehicle into gear, he took one more glance at the rock and focused on three letters at the bottom of the hard surface.

EWD.

1

ATLANTA

"It's not too late," Corin said as she winced against the glare of the afternoon sun.

A foreboding breeze eased across the playground, causing her dark brown hair to flutter behind her ears. Right on cue, a stray cloud in the otherwise crystal-clear sky skirted across the face of the sun, giving the three kids a moment of shade.

"Oh, it's beyond too late," a familiar voice said from behind them.

Diego was the first to spin around, whirling on his feet to face the threat.

Corin and Desmond turned as well, finding themselves closer to the enemy than Diego.

"I've been waiting all summer for this, puke."

Jake stood a few feet away, his freckled face contorted in a menacing scowl.

Two other boys, Jake's cronies, stood just behind him. They were shorter than their leader, even slightly smaller than Diego and his friends. They were known throughout the school as Jake's "pets" due to their undying loyalty to him. Most of the kids at the school didn't find the twins particularly threatening, but they were under the protection of Jake, the biggest kid in the building.

His orange hair blazed like fire in the sunshine as the random cloud dissipated into thin air—it, too, apparently afraid of the freckled bully.

"You haven't been waiting all summer, Jake," Diego corrected with a hint of bravado. He didn't want to get beat up, but he also wasn't going to back down from this guy.

Jake had been running the school with fear and intimidation since the day he first set foot in the sixth grade. He'd be moving on soon, though not soon enough. He had one full year left before going to high school, where many of his classmates hoped their tormentor would meet his match or at least learn a touch of humility.

For now, however, he was standing here right in front of Diego, his stepsister, and his friend, Desmond.

Unbeknownst to Jake and his cronies, they were dealing with a whole different animal than they'd seen throughout the school year.

"What's that supposed to mean, you little pavement stain?" Jake snarled.

"School doesn't start until next week," Diego persisted. "So, maybe you've been waiting for a few months, but not all summer."

"Shut up. You know what I meant." He took a menacing step forward, fingers balling into fists.

Diego and his crew didn't tell the boy that the way he was curling his fingers around the thumbs would result in fractured bones in the digits. That was his problem. Better he figured that out the hard way.

"Sorry for the inconvenience," Diego said. "Maybe you heard. We were in Italy."

"Oh, I saw. You and your little puke friends here think you're something now, huh? Went and got all famous with your treasure hunt in Italy? Well, that means squat here. You're in my town now."

"We don't want any trouble," Corin said, cutting into the conversation.

The tension was unbearable, and she couldn't keep quiet any longer.

"Oh, sending a girl to do your job, Diego?" Jake joked. He turned his head to the other two boys and laughed.

They forced the same guffaw through their lips, though it was easy to tell they didn't think it was funny. In fact, they appeared to be almost afraid of Corin as she narrowed her eyes, flashing them an angry glare. Flames may as well have shot out of her eyes, and the two boys felt themselves involuntarily shuffling a few inches back.

Word of the three friends' exploits in Italy had spread across the globe, reaching their little community just outside of Atlanta. The three bullies knew about what had happened in Rome and the surrounding countryside just a few weeks before.

Corin, Desmond, and Diego had discovered an ancient treasure long thought to be lost to antiquity. The story was featured in global and national news outlets, in papers and on websites just about everywhere.

Jake, however, appeared to be unimpressed.

"Your little friend Wayne isn't here to help you, runt," Jake spat at Diego. "I'm surprised you haven't started running yet."

Diego's eyes flashed angrily. His blood boiled with a confidence unlike anything he'd ever felt before. Something had changed in him during their adventures in Italy. Before that, he'd been timid, shy in almost every social setting. He'd lacked confidence except with his studies as well as with the deep interest he held for history and literature.

In physical confrontations, when his fight-or-flight instincts kicked in, Diego had typically gone the flight route. Running was the only thing he'd ever known, the only way he had for dealing with a crisis like this. And that's exactly what it was: a crisis. To an external observer, someone with no skin in the game, it might have appeared to be just another school squabble.

Except it was much more than that. This was a struggle for power, supremacy in the schoolyard.

And school wasn't even in session yet.

There were still several weeks left of summer vacation, and the three friends had, at Desmond's suggestion, decided to come to the school playground to hang out for an hour or so before heading back home. It was really their parents' fault, Diego and Corin's. They were the ones who insisted the kids go outside and get some exercise, using the age-old motivation that "it was too nice out to stay inside all day."

Kids hated that expression. Hot was hot, and that particular day was sweltering, even by north central Georgia standards.

They'd taken plenty of water in their backpacks, at their mother's behest, and made their way through the neighborhood toward the school. Along the way, they'd taken a wrong turn. To be fair, it wasn't a wrong turn at the time. It was the correct direction, just the wrong moment to take it.

The three had run right into Jake and his two cronies. There would be no escaping now. Jake demanded the three show up at the school in thirty minutes where Diego would get what was coming to him, or so the bully had so ineloquently worded the threat.

If Diego and his friends decided to skip out, they would be branded as chickens for the rest of the school year. Not only that, it was against the kid code to skip out on a fight. Whether you were going to get your tail whipped was irrelevant. The code of the schoolyard demanded attendance by both parties. There was no getting out of it without far worse humiliation than the physical pain Jake could inflict with his fists.

No, the fight was going to happen whether Diego wanted it to or not. He still wasn't sure what he'd done to upset the bully. As far as he knew, nothing. Diego kept his head down most of the time, which might have been the reason Jake picked him out from the throngs of students to be his whipping boy.

It started with name calling in the hall and had gradually escalated to threats of physical harm. The last day of school before summer break, Diego and his stepsister took off, deciding to try to run home instead of meeting Jake at the playground for the proffered fisticuffs.

Diego knew doing so would result in further insult the following year, but it was the choice they'd made, and one that led to a friendship with Desmond and the trip of a lifetime.

But he'd broken the rules of the schoolyard, and now judgment day was upon him. Were he to try to escape again or simply not show up, the verbal bullying he would receive and the disgrace he would have to live with would be unbearable.

No, Diego had no choice.

He and his friends reluctantly made their way to the playground, where they'd hoped to spend some time reading under the shady trees near the picnic tables or chatting about where their next adventure might take them.

Instead, Diego was going to have to go toe to toe with the biggest bully in the school.

All through second semester, Diego had tried to reason with Jake, tried to understand what he'd done to upset the other boy, but it was no use. There was no reasoning with some people, and Jake fell into that category.

"Any last words before I smash your face in, runt?" Jake growled, taking a step forward with fists balled.

Oddly, Diego didn't feel the familiar sense of fear that normally coursed through his veins at a time like this, times when he felt threatened. In the past, he might have cowered and simply taken the punches until the bully tired of the boring fight and decided to trundle off with his two henchmen.

Today, however, Diego felt no fear. It was an alien feeling, a sensation he'd never experienced in a situation like this before, not that he'd been in many fights. Still, he stood his ground, unflinching as Jake bore down on him.

"No. None for me," Diego said dryly. "Do you? Because if you do this, I'm not responsible for what happens."

Corin and Desmond glanced at each other with uncertainty. They'd never heard their friend talk like that with such bravado, such...confidence.

Corin was tempted to tell her brother to back off, to try to use his words to solve whatever problem the bully had with him, but she knew it was no use. The code of the schoolyard was in full force, and there was nothing she could do to stop it. She felt like she was standing next to a railroad track where a massive freight train rumbled toward Diego.

Jake's face contorted at the unexpected comment from the smaller boy, but it didn't stop him fully, only paused his approach. He turned back toward his friends with a crooked grin and chuckled. Then he faced Diego again, the smirk replaced by a fearsome scowl.

"Oh, you're responsible for what happens, all right. You're going to learn some respect, you little rat." He inched forward, ready to strike. "I'm going to enjoy this, Diego. Like they say, the best things come to those who wait."

Jake readied his right fist near his shoulder and shot it forward without further warning.

The entire time the bully was approaching, Diego didn't move, didn't make a motion of any kind. He simply stood there, watching and waiting for the larger boy to make his own move. Sam, the head of security for Desmond's parents, had been working with him and the others over the last few weeks since they'd returned from Italy.

Sam claimed that they needed to learn how to defend themselves in case they ever got into a sticky situation again. He'd warned the kids not to use the skills he taught them as ways to start fights or to attack people. Rather, he wanted the forms to be defensive.

He'd started the three with several different tactical defenses that were easy to learn and easy to deploy against a sloppy assailant. Jake fit every definition of sloppy when it came to his method of attack.

Sam had told the three friends that most of the people they might encounter in the world were untrained, nothing but brawlers with too much confidence and not enough know-how.

Jake clearly fit into that category. Diego had assumed as much, but you could never truly tell until fists started flying.

Diego did as Sam had instructed: quickly analyzed the opponent, picked apart his line of attack, his strategy, his stance, his intent.

Jake was no trained fighter. That much was clear. His chest was too open and his legs too close together, giving Diego plenty of targets to choose if he were to go on the offensive.

Taking the attack to Jake, however, wasn't Diego's plan. He wanted to teach the bully a lesson without having to throw a punch. Luckily, Sam had taught him how to do precisely that.

The fist flew toward Diego's face. For most of the kids in the school, the impending blow would have paralyzed them with fear. The big redheaded bully threw most of his strength behind the punch, hoping to pretty much end the fight in one swift blow.

It was, however, a poor strategy. While it might have worked on most of the terrified kids Jake was accustomed to facing, Diego stood his ground, unflinching in the face of what would probably be an extraordinarily painful shot to the nose or cheek. At the last second, Diego turned his entire body sideways, allowing the now overcommitted Jake to lose his balance. The fist flew by Diego's nose, missing by a good five or six inches. With most of his upper body weight behind the punch, Jake stumbled forward.

Diego stuck out his right foot and caught the other boy on the shin. Jake's momentum and Diego's trip toppled the bully face first to the ground.

The bully managed to land on his hands, but there was an audible pop as he struck the pavement.

Corin's eyes widened, while Desmond couldn't keep from laughing. Even the twins thought it was a little funny but forced back their surprised chuckles lest they also become the target of Jake's ire.

The redhead tried to push himself up, but his left arm gave way and he crumpled back to the ground, screaming in pain. Tears streaked out of the corners of both eyes as he clutched the wounded appendage.

"It's broken! My arm is broken! You broke my arm!" The last accusation fell on deaf ears to Diego and his friends.

Meanwhile, the twins were aghast at what had just happened. They'd come expecting to see a fight, one in which their friend pummeled Diego until he went home crying to his mother. Now, it was Jake that was doing the crying and would—invariably—be the one who ended up crying to his mother.

Right on cue, he yelled at them. "What are you two doing? Help me up!"

The twins snapped into action. They rushed to their leader and hooked their arms under his armpits like they'd seen people do in football games. The two helped Jake to his feet as he continued bawling.

The three shuffled back toward the gate in the fence that led to the street. Jake paused and looked at the three friends still standing there in the middle of the playground. Storms of anger raged in his eyes, but they rained tears down his cheeks, causing the vengeful look to soften considerably.

"I'll get you for this, Diego. You're going to pay for this. You hear me?"

"You should probably get that looked at," Diego said. "If it really is broken, you should be out of the cast by the time school starts."

He knew that wouldn't be the case. While Diego knew relatively little about medical stuff, he'd seen other kids with broken arms before and knew it would be five or six weeks before Jake was out of his cast. That is, if it was indeed broken.

Corin and Desmond sidled up next to their friend as Jake and his rescue squad hobbled off the playground and disappeared around the corner.

When they were gone, Desmond and Corin faced Diego.

"I gotta say, the buildup to that was way more dramatic than the fight." Desmond punched his friend in the shoulder and laughed.

"Yeah, but that was amazing!" Corin added. "I mean, I knew we learned a few things from Sam, but I had no idea it would work so well—and against a bully like Jake."

Diego shrugged. "I just did what Sam said. I could see he was going to be off balance, and so I let him do all the work. Well, that and a little trip didn't hurt."

"It hurt him," Desmond said.

Diego smirked. "Yeah, I guess it did."

"Well, I'm glad that's over with," Corin said.

"Me, too, but maybe we should go somewhere else to hang out for a few hours. You know, leave the scene of the crime?"

"Good call," Desmond agreed. "Come on, let's hit the coffee shop near here. We can get some of those frozen drinks, and then I can show you guys my racing drones."

"Racing drones?" the other two asked in tandem.

Desmond inclined his head. "Yeah. Oh, you guys are about to have your minds blown. You're about to enter the world of FPV drone flight." Flying drones this way made flying a racing or freestyle drone feel like you were actually on the machine.

The three friends went through the same gate Jake and his minions used a few minutes before. Diego followed Desmond and his sister as they turned in the opposite direction of the bullies and made their way down the street.

For the first time in his life, he felt like he could do anything.

2

ATLANTA

Desmond stood at the edge of a huge clearing. The field stretched out for a thousand yards in every direction and was part of a massive park project the county had put together a few years before.

There was a playground for young children, some park benches, picnic tables, and a small amphitheater for occasional weekend concerts that ran from spring to fall. To their right, a gentle slope climbed to a building where a local initiative sponsored a community market every Sunday and showed old movies a couple of times a week. To the left of where the kids stood was a creek that meandered along the edge of the property, surrounded by rows of oaks, poplars, dogwoods, pine, and the occasional maple tree.

The field was perfect for flying a radio-controlled drone, though there weren't many objects to dodge or slalom through. It was perfect for beginners.

Desmond was actually pretty good at flying the high-speed aircraft. He'd been doing it for over a year and even had some freestyle videos on his own YouTube channel.

After picking up their frozen lattes—sans actual coffee—the three went to Desmond's place, picked up three black plastic cases from his workshop in the garage, and then made their way to the area known as the Commons.

There weren't many people there despite it being a spectacular day for being outdoors. There was a little girl flying a kite with her father and mother at the other end of the field, the occasional couple walking down the greenway next to the creek, and several people in their twenties and thirties jogging.

Desmond gripped the controller in his hands and guided the machine through the air with graceful ease. He also had a laptop video feed connected to the drone's transponder, primarily for testing out the signal and quality of the video.

The drone zipped through the sky, buzzing loudly as the four propellers chopped through the air at incredible speed. Desmond sent the machine to the other end of the field, careful not to disturb the girl with the kite and her family, and then flew a massive loop up into the air, nosedived toward the ground, and then bailed out at the last second, leveling the drone expertly before it could smash into the earth.

He spun the machine, barrel-rolling it back up into the sky in a twisting symphony of daring aerobatics, causing his two friends no small amount of unease at the dizzying maneuvers.

Desmond brought the aircraft back around toward them in a steep-angled dive. The three of them could see themselves in the goggles as the machine careened toward them. Desmond laughed as his friends jerked suddenly as though he might actually hit them with the aircraft.

With a flip of his thumbs, the drone slammed to a stop in midair, the props whining loudly as their motors strained under the new command. Then he gently lowered the aircraft to the ground, landing it perfectly on the grass about fifteen feet from where he stood.

"Whoa!" Diego said. He slipped the goggles off of his head and looked down at the drone, then into the goggles, then back at the machine. "That was like...like really flying!"

"It was exhilarating!" Corin exclaimed as she removed her head-set. "Can you teach us how to do that?"

Desmond nodded, beaming proudly. "Of course. And I have a couple of starter drones you can learn with."

"Starter drones?" Diego clearly wasn't okay with the sound of that. He didn't want training wheels. He wanted to do all the tricks Desmond had been doing, experience the same speed his friend's machine displayed.

Desmond chuckled. "Don't worry. They're plenty fast. Not as fast as this one but close. You don't want to start out with the most powerful machine because you're going to crash it."

Diego looked a little hurt by the insinuation. "You don't think I can do it?"

"It's not that," Desmond said with another laugh. "Your first weeks or even months of flying these things is rough. I crashed my first drones dozens of times. Then I started taking it slower, working on specific moves, getting my bearings, and learning every single flight what to do and what not to do."

"Oh," Diego said, understanding but clearly still disappointed.

"Do you still crash now and then?" Corin hedged.

"Oh, absolutely." Desmond set down the controller on his backpack and walked over to the now-dormant drone. "I wrecked this one just before we went to Italy. I had to replace one of the motors, some of the wires. Heck, the first time I built one of these myself, the back-left motor caught on fire."

"It caught fire?" Diego asked, surprised at the revelation.

"Yeah," Desmond laughed. "It was crazy. I was super excited about getting into FPV freestyle flying, and so I went online, bought all the parts I needed, and then set to work."

"How did you know how to do it, the building?" Corin asked.

"YouTube," Desmond said with a shrug. "I watched a bunch of videos on how to do it. There's a guy in Australia that has a bunch of good how-to videos, so I just learned from him. There was a bit of soldering, but with some practice I got better with it. Now I can build one of these in an hour or so."

"That's awesome," Diego said as he eyed his friend's aircraft.

"It's a lot of fun, but I'm not quite good enough to do some of the old abandoned building videos or other intricate structures."

"What do you mean?" Corin asked. "You're good. That was like flying through the air on the quickest motorcycle in the world."

Desmond grinned proudly. "Well, thank you, but I need a lot of practice if I'm going to be able to do some of the stuff I've seen online. Those pilots can take their drones through places I can't. Tight spots, narrow openings in walls or corridors...I even saw one guy flying one through an old ventilation shaft in an abandoned warehouse. There's another one where this dude zips it through a parking garage and can flip it over so it's flying sideways for a second just so he could get it through a balcony railing."

"If I tried something like that, I would lose my drone for sure," Diego said, disheartened.

"I came close once, which is why I still come out here to practice." Desmond waved a hand around. "This place is perfect for learning because if you crash it into the grass, no big deal. Maybe have to fix a few things, but you won't lose your drone unless you happen to land it on that roof over there or maybe get too close to the trees. Typically, I try to avoid the trees unless I'm working on slaloms. Even then, those trees are smaller, and I stick to weaving around the trunks."

"Well, I'm sure you're going to be one of the best soon enough," Corin encouraged.

"Thanks," Desmond said, a little embarrassed.

"Have you ever used your drone just to take video footage of other places? You know, flying over water or the city at night?"

"A little, but you have to be careful about these things. I typically wouldn't advise doing it in the city or over a crowded area, just in case something went wrong with the aircraft. And most of the drones that do those kinds of things are bigger quad copters, or they might even be an octo copter with eight props. They're slower, bulkier, and have higher-end cameras on them specifically for taking professional video and photos. I've flown a few of those before and they can be fun, but there's nothing like this. Like you said, it's a lot like riding a speeding motorcycle in the air. A motorcycle that can do flips and stop, turn, and accelerate almost instantly."

He looked around the area and then checked his watch. "So, you guys ready to try it out?"

The two siblings glanced at each other and then faced him again with eager eyes. They nodded excitedly.

"Cool. Let's get you set up."

Desmond produced two more drones from additional cases he'd brought along and controllers from two other bags.

"Normally, I would have a small table with me to keep these organized, but we didn't drive here today, and I'm not walking around with a plastic table."

The other two laughed.

He grinned appreciatively and then continued. "This one," he pointed to a carbon fiber quad in the shape of an X, "is my dragon."

"Dragon?" Diego asked, staring at the black chassis with bright red supports and props.

Desmond nodded, waiting to see if they would make the connection.

"Oh," Corin realized. "This is the one that caught fire?"

"Boom," Desmond said. "You got it. Yep. This is the first one I built."

"Doesn't look like it's damaged," Diego said, tilting his head to get a better look. He clearly wasn't convinced that this drone had ever been on fire.

"There is some scoring under that tie-down there," He pointed under a set of wires that ran along the length of one of the quad's arms. "Most of the damage was to the wiring and the wire coating. I had to replace the flight controller, the wires, even decided to change the motors, too, just in case. That first time, the thing only got about two inches off the ground before it burst into flames."

"What caused that to happen?" Corin asked, always curious about the science behind almost everything.

"I went online and found that some of the parts for that particular drone were made with less than optimal quality control. Could have been anything: a fleck of dust got in during the production process, or maybe the materials were so cheap they couldn't handle the power surging through them. Either way, I upgraded the tech so that wouldn't happen again. So far, it hasn't."

"Still, that sounds kind of dangerous."

Desmond rolled his shoulders nonchalantly. "I did some research and found it's a pretty common problem with those specific components. They should come with a warning, though. I mean, it's not like you're going to try to fly one of these in your house, but if it caught fire in a dry field like this one, say, after a drought, you'd have some big fires on your hands. That day I was testing it out on the driveway, so it was no biggie. Still, a little crazy."

"No doubt."

Desmond set about getting the other two set up with their aircraft and then went through the instructions of how to fly the machines.

The first flight for both the siblings was less than spectacular. While their seasoned pilot friend made it look easy, the two of them struggled to get their drones to fly straight or even hover in place for very long. They crashed several times before the batteries died— which only lasted for five or six minutes at most. None of the wrecks were catastrophic to the drones, since Desmond had taken precautions to protect them against beginner mistakes.

Once they'd used up all the batteries Desmond had brought along, it was time to go home for the day.

The three walked back to Desmond's house, where he asked if they'd like to stay for dinner. Corin and Diego had to decline due to a prior commitment with their own family dinner.

After the three said their goodbyes, Diego and Corin made their way back to their own home, where they stepped into the house to the aromas of onions, spices, and beef.

There was a good reason they'd turned down Desmond's offer of dinner at the Ellerbys. While it would have been unquestionably fancier than what they would receive at home, there was no comparison when it came to Maria Townsend's taco night.

Diego had grown up with his mother's tacos, tortas, enchiladas, and other homemade Mexican dishes. Corin had been adopted into Maria's cooking traditions when her father and Diego's mom got together. While there were many things she appreciated about her new family, the food was probably in her top five. Maybe top three.

"Hey, kids," their father said from the kitchen.

They hung their bags on coat hooks near the door and closed the entrance before too much cool air left the house. Summers were brutal in Atlanta, and every bit of air conditioning they could keep in the house was an almost priceless commodity. For decades, parents of Southern children could be heard yelling the same phrase through open doorways or windows. "Close that! Are you trying to air-condition the entire neighborhood?"

Diego and Corin had been no exception to that habit and had learned quickly to close doors immediately after they entered the house.

"Smells great, as always, Mom," Diego said to his mother over the sizzle of beef in a frying pan.

"Oh, thank you, honey. Did you two have fun?"

Diego ambled into the kitchen with his sister right behind him.

"Yeah, Desmond showed us how to fly FPV racing drones today."

Dad looked up from where he was chopping green onions on a section of the wooden island. His brow was wrinkled in confusion. "What? What's FPB?"

"FPV," Corin corrected. "It means first-person view."

"Oh." Their dad went back to cutting up the garnishing and then moved on to a ripe tomato by his left hand. "So, what does that mean?"

Corin chuckled at her dad's ignorance. "You put on special goggles to fly the thing. It makes it feel like you're on board the drone."

"There's a camera on the front and a radio transmitter that sends a signal to your goggles. So, it's very realistic. Desmond is incredible at it. He can do all sorts of tricks and aerobatics."

"And he let you fly it?" Mom asked.

"No," Corin said cheerfully. "He had a few beginner models for us. Probably for the best since we ended up crashing them several times."

"Oh dear. I hope you didn't break Desmond's toys."

"They're not toys," Diego defended. "I mean, they're kind of toys, but still. Not in the normal sense of the word. Anyway, we didn't break anything. He built them himself, and they can take a beating. Desmond's, though, was flying super fast. He said that some of the faster drones can reach speeds of 90 miles per hour. And he also said there are some coming out soon that can go even faster."

"Wow," their dad said. "That's pretty impressive. Are these the same kinds of drones we see doing real-estate videos and stuff like that?"

"No," Diego answered. "I wondered the same thing, but Desmond said those are slower. They're built for longer flight times but not speed."

"Interesting," Mom chimed in.

"Yeah, it was awesome."

"So, what else did you two do today?" She continued to stir the beef in a large frying pan. Steam wafted up from the pan in rolling clouds, filling the house with the savory smell of meat and spices.

The two kids looked at each other. Trepidation filled their eyes, and they weren't sure how much, if anything, they should tell their mother about the fight in the schoolyard with Jake the bully.

They'd already discussed it on the way home, knowing that such questions would be forthcoming from their parents. Their mom and dad always asked what they'd done that day, what they'd learned in school, or what shenanigans they might have gotten themselves into. It wasn't that their parents didn't trust them. They honestly cared about their kids and their day-to-day activities. The inquiry came more from a point of genuine interest than paranoia.

"Nothing worth mentioning," Diego offered.

His parents seemed to accept the answer and went back to finishing dinner.

"Well, go upstairs, and wash up. Dinner will be ready in ten minutes."

The two kids nodded, relieved they'd gotten off the hook, and scurried up the stairs to their respective rooms.

Washing up pretty much just consisted of getting their hands clean, but with nine minutes to spare, the two siblings took the free time to make sure they weren't going to tell their parents about the fight with Jake earlier that day. Diego was in his room, sitting down at his desk to use his computer for a minute when Corin walked in.

"Hey, I just wanted to double-check. We're not going to tell them about the fight, right?" Corin asked.

"It wasn't a fight," Diego defended with a hint of snark in his voice. "Not a real fight. I mean, if Jake fought anyone, it was the pavement. From the looks of it, he lost." Diego's mouth curled in a devilish grin.

"You know what I mean," Corin groused. "We telling them or not?"

He jerked his head back and forth. "No. Probably best not to."

"It's a shame," Corin said.

His eyebrows lowered in confusion. "How so?"

Her lips curled into a grin. "You did good."

"Well."

"Well what?"

"You did well. That's what you...never mind."

She rolled her eyes. "I'm giving you a compliment, Diego. Just roll with it. Okay? No need to correct my English."

He snorted a laugh. "Sorry. And thank you. I don't know what came over me. I've never felt that...brave before."

She crossed her arms. "Well, it suits you. And I'm proud of you. You stood up for yourself."

His tanned face darkened with a slight blush. "Thanks."

"What you doing?" she asked, changing the subject before it got awkward.

"Oh nothing. Just checking email real quick."

She nodded and turned to leave. "Don't be long, or I may not save you any tacos." Corin disappeared into the hallway as Diego, with a chuckle, turned to face his computer screen.

3

ATLANTA

Diego stared at the screen, looking through the scraps of email filling the inbox. Most of it was unimportant, which was—he realized—normal for a boy his age. Although most of the kids his age weren't using email for the same thing he was, those who did have email accounts were using them simply to sign up for social media apps or to get accounts on YouTube and other applications. Diego didn't care much for that stuff, except for YouTube. He'd learned so much from that site over the years, and he mentally made a note to come back to YouTube after dinner to check out some of the drone freestyle videos he'd heard about from Desmond.

He scrolled through the short list of legitimate emails and spotted one from Wayne Collins.

Diego's lips creased happily as he clicked the message from the man who had, at one point earlier that summer, been an enemy. Now, the two communicated back and forth about different artifacts, mysteries that remained unsolved from long ago, and general history. Diego's parents had been informed about the communication between the two since the beginning and also had access to Diego's account to make sure he was safe at all times.

The second Diego saw the subject of the email, he had to open it. It read, "Have you seen this?!"

The mini box opened to display the message, and Diego began reading. He imagined he was sitting in a lavish study somewhere in London, which was likely where Wayne had compiled the email.

Hello, my young friend. I hope you and your friends are well. I've had an interesting couple of weeks here in London and finally had a chance to sit down to do a little investigating.

There was something that's always bothered me in terms of American history, and now my curiosity is higher than ever.

After that intro, so was Diego's.

I'm not sure if you've studied this yet in school, but back in the 1500s—when the United States was still just a group of colonies—there was a bizarre mystery that has, to this day, baffled historians and investigators.

Yep, Wayne sure knew how to hook a kid's interest, Diego's at least.

There was a colony established on the coast of North Carolina in a place called Roanoke on what is now known as the Outer Banks. In 1587, John White, the governor of the colony, was sent back to England to gather more supplies for the settlement.

His timing couldn't have been worse. When he arrived in Europe, a naval war broke out between England and Spain. Queen Elizabeth I summoned every ship the nation could spare to fight against the mighty Spanish Armada.

The result was that John White was forced to stay in England for three years until ships were available for passage back to the colonies.

By the time White returned, he found all 115 of the colonists missing, including his wife, his daughter, and his granddaughter, Virginia Dare, who was an infant when he left and the first English child born in the colonies.

White searched everywhere for the people but found nothing. Not a trace of what happened to them—save for one thing. The word CROA-TOAN was carved into one of the trees in the settlement.

Some people thought that meant the colonists had been abducted by the local Croatoan natives to an island off the coast that was thought to be their domain. That search turned out fruitless, as well.

In the end, no one found out anything, and John White lived out the rest of his life wondering what must have happened to his family.

It's a sad story.

That's an understatement, thought Diego.

For centuries, historians, archaeologists, and even tourists have tried to understand what could have possibly happened to 115 people that caused them to simply vanish from the face of the earth.

One clue has emerged in the search for answers. It's called the Dare Stone. It was found in North Carolina, far away from the coast where the Roanoke Colony was established. This stone, however, tells a strange tale. It was written in the English of the day, which means the spellings are strange and difficult to read.

"Diego! Corin!" His mother's voice boomed up the staircase and into his bedroom. "Dinner's ready! You two come down and eat, please!"

"Okay, Mom!" Diego shouted back. "Be right down!"

"Me, too! Coming!" Corin added.

From the other end of the hall, she saw Diego staring at his computer screen. "Hey, tacos, Brother."

He didn't take his eyes off the monitor. "Yeah. Yeah. Be right down." The absent tone in his voice told her he was focused on whatever he was reading on the screen.

Corin decided not to push it and bounded down the stairs, her feet clomping on every step as she descended.

Diego kept reading, hoping to finish the email before he had used up all his grace period with his parents, especially his mother.

The stone speaks of many deaths. One of which was Virginia Dare's child; another was her husband. There were others, some from attacks by natives. The carvings go on to suggest that the settlers who remained alive were forced to leave Roanoke. It's difficult to tell if it's saying they had to escape or simply moved peaceably.

There are a couple of fascinating pieces to this, though.

The first is that some of the message suggests that evil spirits were there, both driving some of the colonists mad and possessing many of the local natives, which was believed to be the cause of some of the attacks.

The second, and extremely interesting, part is that it was signed EWD, the initials of Eleanor White Dare, the daughter of the governor, John White.

Diego felt goose bumps rise across his arms and the back of his neck. This was getting good.

"Diego, come downstairs, please. We're waiting." His mom's second order was more serious than the first. He knew if she had to call for him a third time he'd be in trouble. At the very least, Corin and his father would be irritated at him for making them wait to scarf down some of his mom's famous tacos.

"On my way, Mom!" he replied, slowly rising from his seat as he finished reading the email from Wayne.

There were other stones reportedly discovered, but all of them have been largely discounted as fakes created by opportunists trying to make a little money on something they're passing off as historic and valuable. Still, the first Dare Stone is worth a look if you ever get the chance. And since it's kept at Brenau University, not far from where you are in Atlanta, you may be able to persuade your parents to take you over there for a day to have a look.

Just a thought. I know you love this kind of stuff, so I thought I would send it to you. Maybe there's a mystery there for you and your friends to solve.

Well, I'm off on another adventure. To the supermarket. Ha!

Have a great day.
Your friend,
Wayne

Diego didn't bother closing his laptop as he stepped toward the door. He didn't have time. Any second, his mother would be calling for the third time, the time he knew would lead to a less than pleasurable evening.

He rounded the corner and let his footfalls hit hard on the steps so his parents would hear him coming and know that he wasn't still in his room. He appeared around the corner of the wall at the bottom of the steps and bounded down the final two and into the foyer then spun around the banister and hurried to the kitchen in the back of the house.

His family was already seated at the table. Corin had three tacos on her plate, loaded and ready to go with cheese, lettuce, tomato, and beef. Mom and Dad were both working on their own taco construction.

"Sorry," Diego said. "I was reading an email from Mr. Collins."

"Oh?" His mother didn't seem to be irritated that he'd taken so long to get down to the dining area. That was a positive.

"What did he have to say?" Dad asked.

Corin looked up eagerly awaiting the answer, though her cheeks bulged with a mouthful of taco bites she was still chewing.

Diego slid into his seat and scooped up a plate, filling it with three taco shells of his own. He answered Dad's question as he shoveled beef into the shells. "Now and then, we email each other about stuff we find on the internet or in books or magazines—occasionally, television shows, too. Apparently, he found something he thought was interesting about the Lost Colony of Roanoke."

Their mom and dad looked up from their plates and shared a glance that neither Diego nor Corin could describe. It was one of... worry? Confusion?

Diego decided to go on. "Anyway, he was telling me about this thing called the Dare Stone that's apparently kept at Brenau University. That's not far from here, is it?"

Dad was the first to snap out of it. "No. Not far at all. And yes, the Dare Stones are quite the infamous artifacts." He held up his fingers and used air quotes to highlight the final word.

"Most of those were discredited a long time ago, honey," his mom added.

"I know," he said with a nod. "That's what Mr. Collins said. He mentioned it in his email."

"Did he?"

"Yep." Diego took a spoon from a bowl of white cheddar cheese and sprinkled the shreds onto each of the three tacos, then added some lettuce from a nearby plate. "He said that the only legitimate stone was the original one found by some guy in the 1930s. Pretty crazy, huh?"

Dad nodded. "Yes. It's crazy, all right."

"And you said that stone is at Brenau?" Corin asked, ignoring her dad's barb.

"That's what Mr. Collins told me. Said it might be fun to look into it. Could we go to Brenau and have a look at it?" He asked his mother. "You guys probably have connections with people at the university. We could drive over there one day, maybe this weekend, have a look, then come back."

His mom chewed her taco slowly. She nodded at a pace that matched the movement of her jaw and lips. "Yeah, I suppose that's possible."

"Really?" Diego's voice chirped with excitement.

"Sure," Mom said. "But we are not driving to Roanoke. That's a long drive from here, and your father and I are running fourth summer session at the college."

Diego nodded in understanding. His parents only had a month or so off every year since they taught classes in the fall and spring, then again at the tail end of summer. The extra work provided them with some additional funds for things like vacations during fall break and at the beginning of summer. Without the money from those summer sessions, the family might never do anything fun together.

"Okay," Diego said. "Would it be okay if we took Desmond, too? I think he'd enjoy it."

Dad's head bobbed in assent. "Sure. Bring him along. In fact, I don't think we have any plans this weekend. We could drive over there on Saturday and take a look. I think we may have a connection in the history department there, although last I checked they had several of the stones on display. Even some the ones that were deemed illegitimate."

"Awesome. I mean, not the ones that are fakes, but you know, if they have the real one there for us to see, that would be epic."

"Okay, then," Mom chimed after swallowing a big bite of taco. "It sounds like we're going to Brenau this weekend."

"Sweet," Corin said.

"Yes, but like we said," Dad reminded, "whatever you may find or learn there, don't get it in your heads that we're going to drive to Roanoke. Now, if you two want to trade your Disney vacation this fall for a trip to Roanoke, we can do that."

He let the words hang for a moment to reinforce the seriousness of the consequences.

"No," the two kids said simultaneously.

"Disney is still good," Diego said. In his head, though, he was already trying to think of a way that he and the other two members of the Adventure Guild could get to North Carolina. As far as he knew, his parents didn't have any plans for the next few weeks leading into the beginning of the new school year. That meant taking a little trip with, say, the Ellerbys might be possible.

For now, though, that would have to wait. There was no sense in putting together grand schemes when he hadn't even seen the Dare Stone yet. They would need to analyze the inscription first. And that still didn't guarantee they'd be able to figure anything out. After all, they were just three middle school kids. Those stones had probably been pored over hundreds of times in the last century alone. What could he and his friends find that the best minds in archaeology couldn't?

Diego wasn't sure, but the confidence he'd felt earlier in the day when confronting Jake still coursed through his veins. Was this the start of another adventure? Surely not, though a creeping feeling in his mind told him that anything was possible.

4

GAINESVILLE, GEORGIA

Anton Schneider watched as the campus safety truck pulled into the parking lot. The driver guided the vehicle slowly through the lot as he scanned the area for trouble.

Anton sighed with impatient derision as the pickup truck's driver paused a few times to check his phone, probably a text message from some girl he was trying to impress with his uniform and fake badge. He imagined the security guy was sending her something macho, talking about how he was "on duty" or using some other terminology Anton couldn't conceive to be remotely legitimate. Still, he had to stay out of sight.

Even the lights on the truck were fake, a bright green that would probably strike laughter instead of fear in the hearts of anyone trying to get away with something on campus. Were the driver to turn them on, a less cautious criminal might even be inclined to laugh.

Anton didn't fear the campus security officer, but the truck's driver would certainly have a phone. Phones could contact backup. Backup with guns. That was something Anton had no intention of dealing with on this night.

He continued watching until the security guard exited the

parking lot and continued down the campus street toward the next set of buildings.

"Looks like he's gone," Anton said to his associate crouching next to him behind another private study desk.

Gunter Becker nodded. "Right. So, we make our move now, yes?"

Anton inclined his head in confirmation. "Yes. We make our move now. Come."

The two German men had snuck into the library earlier in the afternoon, going in through the back door so as not to attract attention from the librarians at the front desk. It had been easy enough to hang out, pretending to do research with stacks of books surrounding them until it was time for the staff to close the doors for the night.

The three librarians on duty were hardly a thorough security unit. The women meandered through the mazes of shelves, desks, and computers, giving barely more than a vague glance down the rows and into the alcoves as they proceeded through their mundane nightly routine.

Anton and Gunter left their hiding spot and continued to the back of the library where they took cover behind a row of bookshelves packed tight with dusty tomes. A security camera at the corner, hovering over a study nook, looked down on the area silently. Its red light indicated the device was recording and likely sending a live signal back to wherever the university's campus security headquarters was located. Or perhaps the feed went straight to some library-centered security room, though that was doubtful.

Anton briefly wondered if the security device was even real. He knew that most retail stores displayed camera domes all over ceilings, but what the general public didn't realize was that many of those cameras within the darkly tinted domes were actually fake. Using dummy cameras was one of the three pillars of defending against theft, that pillar being *deter*. Deterring a potential crime was just as good as catching someone in the act. Dummy cameras were deployed at high ratios, based on what Anton had learned, and there were—at any given time—only a certain number of domes that used real cameras.

In this case, Anton wasn't going to take any chances. They'd already disarmed the security system the second the last librarian left the building. She'd set the alarm and exited through the front door while the system counted down with a series of beeps.

Anton and Gunter both knew they had two minutes from the time the alarm was set. After that, the motion detectors positioned in every corner of the building would pick up movement. Sure, there were places they could sneak around without triggering an alarm, but those were in the center of the library. What they were there for wasn't in that location. It was in a place that the university protected more vigilantly.

It had been easy enough to deactivate the library alarm system. Anton had developed a device that could override almost any basic system such as the one this library used. There were, of course, more complex systems in place, but he knew those weren't here on this campus, at least not in the main section of the library.

Gunter withdrew a small circular photograph from his back pocket and applied a piece of tape to the top. Then he climbed up the shelves nearest the camera, careful not to knock any books off or tip the thing over. Once he was at the top of the shelf, he reached out over a gap between himself and the camera, using his left hand to brace his weight. His right hand quickly attached the image to the camera lens, securing it perfectly over the circular glass.

The image was of the library, a photo of the exact angle they'd procured in the weeks before leading up to their break-in.

Sure, the guys back at the security office might see the flicker on the screen as Gunter placed the photo in place, but it was doubtful at best. They weren't seasoned mercenaries, former special forces, or some kind of super spies that would always be on alert. In fact, it was doubtful anyone was paying attention to the monitors. It wouldn't be until later, when the university's most prized archaeological possession was missing, that they would go back and try to analyze the video footage to find out what happened.

The only thing they would see would be a slight irregularity in the image. By the time investigators discovered the photo taped to the lens, Anton and Gunter would be long gone, and there would be no trace of who was responsible for the crime.

Gunter carefully descended the shelf with the skill of a monkey. His gangly, skinny frame made him perfect for such operations, while Anton was more of the brute, a hulking man ripped with muscles from long days in the gym. He wasn't a bodybuilder, but the man was definitely the stronger of the two, slightly taller, as well.

Anton's concerns had been minimal.

Once Gunter was on the floor next to him, the two men moved toward the doors leading into the special collections section of the library.

They paused at the doors and waited for a moment, double-checking to make sure the alarms were off. The two had done their homework, researching blueprints and other schematics to learn whether the special collections section of the library had its own security system, which it did not.

However, there were other dangers that could ensnare the two men if they were careless. For example, the door leading into the special collections room was connected to the main security system, which they'd already deactivated, but that hardly meant they were out of the woods.

Within the chamber housing the famous Dare Stones were more security cameras, each positioned to cover every square inch of the room. And Anton and Gunter knew those cameras would be working. The second the two men went in, they would be on camera and there was nothing they could do about that, unless of course they decided to change plans and go in through a window. That, however, would be just as bad. The windows were locked, and while Anton and his associate were skilled at picking locks and getting into tight places, this wasn't the time to go trying that sort of thing.

First of all, the windows were old, which meant opening them at all might prove problematic. Anton had seen it before when he'd tried to break into a records office of an old building in Stuttgart. The windows hadn't budged, and he nearly got himself nabbed by the police, narrowly escaping down a side street while the cops wasted their time scouring the inside of the building.

No, windows were too unpredictable. Now that they were inside, there was no turning back.

Luckily, they had a trick up their sleeve for this particular contingency.

"Flash and smoke it," Anton ordered.

Gunter acknowledged with a curt nod and reached into a pouch in the utility belt around his waist. He retrieved two discs. One was black and the other silver.

He pressed on the silver one first, tapping it five times so that the micro detonator within wouldn't go off until five seconds had passed. Then he crouched low and slid the disc under the gap between the door and the floor.

The metal object slid to the center of the room where one of the Dare Stones was on display. The tiny disc struck the plinth and bounced a few inches away.

As the clock ticked down inside Gunter's head, he rapidly tapped the second disc two times and then flung the thing into the room as he had the first.

Before the black disc reached the other, a bright flash of searing white light streaked through the room. The mini flash-bang device would easily knock out the cameras within the chamber, but it would also catch the attention of security, if there were any sitting around watching the monitors.

In Anton's mind, that was a fifty-fifty proposition, but it didn't matter. He had no intention of sticking around long.

The second disc erupted in a cloud of white smoke that billowed out of the tiny thing and rose toward the ceiling, filling the once-secure room. The flash of the first device would temporarily knock out the cameras, causing them to essentially reset themselves. It wouldn't take more than ten seconds to occur, but the smoke would keep the lenses effectively blind for several minutes. That was more than enough time for Anton and Gunter.

The two Germans pushed through the doors and into the fog on the other side. They moved cautiously. If they accidentally destroyed the stone, then their entire plan, the whole operation, would be for nothing.

Anton was the first to find a display case in the haze. The room overflowed with the thick smoke, and were it not for the masks the two intruders were wearing, they would have been forced to exit and return after clearing their lungs.

A quick look told Anton he wasn't at the correct display, so he moved on, finding another just a short distance away. Again, it wasn't the authentic stone but one of the fakes that had been created after the craze of the first stone.

The men maneuvered through the special collections room with care, but after searching through several display cases, they were still empty-handed. And now, the smoke was starting to clear.

Anton knew they would only have one shot at this. Should they fail, the university would certainly up their level of security immediately. Once that happened, getting into this place would be nearly impossible. They might even take the stone somewhere else or put it in a vault. The job would never get any easier than it was on this night. He had to get the stone now, or it could fall out of his grasp forever.

A thought occurred to him, and he dropped down to his knees, positioning himself on all fours. From this vantage point, the air was clearer, which made sense since the smoke was constantly rising, seeking escape from its prison in the room.

He could see all the display cases now, though much of the upper part containing the glass and the stones within were still shrouded in the dissipating mist.

There. He saw it. The display case that held the original Dare Stone, the one known as the Chowan River Stone.

He snapped a finger and drew Gunter's attention. His subordinate jerked his head in Anton's direction and saw his boss down on the floor. He immediately dropped down into the same position and bear-crawled over to him.

Anton pointed at the display holding the Chowan River Stone

and started forward. He scurried quickly under the rising smoke. He reached the case and stood, careful that the dark mask covering his face was still pulled high, all the way up to the top of his cheekbones. His eyes, too, were covered in lightly tinted goggles. No one would be able to identify him or Gunter should even a moment of video capture the two thieves.

Anton stared at the stone for a moment, admiring it through the haze. This was it, the item he'd been searching for so long. He hadn't known it would be this, the infamous Dare Stone. It took him years to pinpoint exactly which artifact he needed to go with the other one, but now the code would be completed. With this stone, he would be able to decipher the mystery of what happened to the Lost Colony of Roanoke—and harness the same power that caused their end.

He reached down to his hip and drew a black metal club from its sheath. The thing was weighty in his right hand and caused his forearm to flex involuntarily.

Sirens echoed in the distance. Someone *had* been watching the cameras. It was no matter. The alarm was going to be set off anyway. The fact that the police were already on their way changed nothing. Actually, it made the decision to obliterate the glass case that much easier.

Anton swung the weapon at the case. The glass shattered into thousands of pieces, spraying across the room and onto the floor.

He sheathed the club and reached out with both hands to remove the stone. His fingers wrapped around the hard edges of each side, and he lifted it. The thing was heavy, just over twenty pounds, and the angle he had to use to pick it up made the muscles in his arms and back strain. Anton handled it, though, and turned with the stone in his hands to face Gunter.

His henchman was holding a black nylon bag that was lined with fleece on the inside. Anton lowered the stone into the bag and then zipped it shut.

Gunter strapped it onto his back, and the two men immediately exited through the door leading into the main floor of the library.

Outside, blue lights flashed against the other buildings on campus and off of the leaves of trees that dotted the quad.

Gainesville was a small town, but even they were overstocked with police officers, and a robbery at the library of Brenau University would be something that brought every uniformed cop within fifteen miles to the scene of the crime.

This would be a big deal to the entire town, including the police department.

The two men made their way to the back door, where they had entered and pried it open, only allowing enough of a gap to peek through. There were no cops at the rear of the building, but that would change soon enough. Anton knew they were screeching to a stop on the street out front and in the adjacent parking lot.

Even with a head start, it wouldn't be long before the cops were able to zero in on their escape route, which was why Anton had a contingency plan.

Before they arrived at the library, he and Gunter had strolled through the campus, dressed like ordinary professionals. They were likely perceived as professors walking from building to building.

With so few witnesses on campus during the summer months, it was easy to navigate the property without raising suspicion. Their stroll, however, was with a purpose.

Anton and Gunter had planted small explosive devices on low-hanging tree branches, behind bushes, and everywhere they could think of. The explosives weren't powerful. In fact, they were little more than powder extracted from firecrackers and compacted into little plastic tubes. The damage they could do to a tree or bush would be negligible, probably little more than a black scorch mark. If held in a human hand, they would certainly have enough punch to blow off some fingers and do permanent damage to the appendage.

In this case, hurting someone wasn't the goal. These little explosives were a diversion.

Anton reached into his vest and removed a small black box. It was about the size of a cell phone and nearly as thick. He slid the thing open, revealing four red buttons and a tiny switch within. He flipped the switch and then waited for a moment, listening for the sounds of cops shouting orders. When he glanced back and saw that the police were surrounding the front of the building, he pressed the first button.

Sounds like gunshots rang out through the night, echoing across the campus in what sounded like an all-out gunfight. The loud pops could be heard through the property, and the buildings seemed to cause the reverberation to be louder, sending the quiet university campus into a kind of cacophony that could have easily been mistaken for a war zone.

Anton narrowed his eyes and waited. Then he pressed the second button. More pops started from the diversionary explosives. Cops' voices mingled with the chaos as the officers in charge shouted commands to pursue the gunmen.

He and Gunter couldn't see them from their vantage point in the rear of the library, but they knew the police would chase the sounds of the "gunfire," which just happened to be the opposite direction the thieves were going.

The two men stepped out of the back door and into the warm summer night. Anton pressed the third button, and again, more detonations led the cops farther away from the real targets. Anton waited until they were at least a hundred yards clear of the library before he pressed the last button.

By the time the last of the explosives sounded, they were well beyond the lights of the campus, save for the flashing blue lights that reflected off of the trees, dorms, and buildings.

They reached their vehicle that was parked innocuously next to a collection of park benches near a creek. The men gave little concern for the pursuit that was happening on campus.

Clear of any danger, the two quickly changed out of their tactical gear and into the clothes they'd worn earlier in the day, donning disguises of well-learned professors. Then, they drove away, leaving Brenau and the city of Gainesville behind without a clue as to who had been there, and why they could possibly want the first of the Dare Stones.

5

ATLANTA

The next morning, Diego woke with a start and shot up out of his bed. He looked around the room at his posters of cars, sports figures, and favorite historic locations from all over the globe. His computer sat idle on the desk, the screen dark and in sleep mode.

Nothing in his room had been touched, but he had the distinct feeling that something was wrong. He glanced over at the door and saw that it was just as he'd left it the night before. It was closed shut and unlocked.

He rested his head against the headboard for a moment, rubbed his eyes with both hands, and then sighed. After another minute of waking up, he swung his legs over the edge of the bed and planted his feet on the cool floor.

His parents kept the house at a chilly sixty-eight degrees each night, which was good for sleeping but brutal to wake up to each day.

He shuffled across the room, slipped into his pajama pants, and then meandered down the stairs where the aromas of fresh coffee melted with potatoes and onions cooking in a skillet.

Diego rounded the bottom of the banister and found his father cooking hash browns and scrambled eggs. A plate of toast sat in the center of the table, along with two kinds of butter—dairy and non.

"Good morning," Diego said as he entered the kitchen and walked to the fridge.

"Morning, Son," Dad said.

"Where's Mom?"

"She's getting ready for work. We have new students coming in today for advisement regarding the upcoming semester."

"What about you?" Diego asked as he opened the fridge and took out a bottle of grape juice. He set the bottle on the counter and retrieved a tall skinny glass from the cabinet and began pouring the dark purple juice into the container.

Dad glanced with a mischievous grin over his shoulder at his stepson. "I'm already ready," he said in a whisper.

Diego snorted a laugh and shook his head. "Okay, then."

He put the grape juice back in the fridge and set the glass down at an empty seat at the table.

"Your sister up yet?"

"Dunno," the boy shrugged and snagged a piece of wheat toast. He placed it on the plate and scooped up some of the nondairy butter, spread it on the bread with a butter knife, and then took a bite.

"Yeah, I'm up," Corin said, bounding down the last two steps on the staircase. "Why?"

"Just asking," Dad said. "Because the eggs and taters are done."

He shoveled a load of the golden hash browns onto a plate. He repeated the process until the skillet was empty, and then he spun and set the plate on the table. Next, he deftly whipped around and did the same thing with the eggs, sliding them onto another plate and then serving it up with a pinch of salt and pepper.

"Bon appétit," he said with hands out wide.

The kids didn't wait for another invitation to eat. They scooped the eggs and potatoes out onto their plates and combined them with some of the toast.

Dad asked Corin if she wanted juice, and when she said yes he poured her a glass similar to Diego's and set it next to her plate while he leaned back against the counter, sipping his cup of black coffee.

Footsteps down the hallway signaled that their mother was

coming, and the two turned in time to see her as she appeared around the corner.

Her hair was pulled back into a tight ponytail. She wore fitted black slacks, a pale blue blouse that had a ruffled seam down the center, and shiny black shoes.

She was the opposite of her husband, who appeared to be content with walking into the halls of the college with nothing more than a pair of khakis and a white button-up T-shirt.

The two kids had heard the *is that what you're wearing* argument more times than they could count, though it had been a while. They figured it must have worn off over time and that, eventually, their mother had given up the cause.

Mom smiled at them as she entered and walked straight for the coffee pot, where her husband was still leaning against the edge of the counter. He twisted slightly, dipping his hand behind him for a moment. Then he produced another mug, this one full to the top with steaming, light brown liquid.

"One cream, one sugar. Just like you like it," he said with a proud grin.

Mom took the mug gratefully and eased into a chair near Corin. She sipped the cup and nodded. "Perfect, honey, as usual."

Dad afforded himself a thin smile and continued drinking his coffee.

The kids weren't sure why their father always made the coffee, but they had their suspicions. Whenever he was out of town and it was only Mom there, she complained about the coffee as if there was nothing she could do about it. She said it wasn't as good as what their father made, and so whenever he was gone she typically went to one of the local coffee shops and ordered some java to go.

She placed some of the eggs and potatoes on her plate and then grabbed a piece of toast, opting to use a little of the real butter for it. As she chewed the first bite, Mom took out her phone and looked through the news feed.

Her brow furrowed, the eyebrows tightening over her nose as she read something on the screen that apparently disturbed her. "Oh my," she said, as if the look on her face wasn't enough to convey that exact thought.

"What is it?" Dad asked first.

"Hold on," she said, putting up a finger to reiterate she needed a few more moments to investigate whatever it was that had caught her attention with such an iron grip.

Dad stepped away from the counter and slid into a seat across from her.

"It's the Dare Stone," she said. "Someone broke into the library at Brenau last night and took the original Dare Stone."

"The Chowan River one?" Dad asked.

"Yeah," she nodded absently, still scouring the screen for more information.

Diego looked at her, forlorn. Then he started chuckling. "Yeah, right. I'm not stupid, Mom. I know you're kidding. It's not very funny, by the way."

She shook her head, and her expression didn't change. "I'm not kidding, Son," she said and turned her phone toward him so he could see it.

Corin leaned over to get a better look, too.

Sure enough, the phone displayed an article about the stolen arti-fact. There was a picture of yellow police tape surrounding the library at Brenau and several Gainesville police officers standing around in the background.

The headline read, "Famous Dare Stone Stolen."

"I...I don't understand," Diego sputtered. Suddenly, he wasn't so hungry, and he felt his stomach turning.

"I don't, either, which is why I'm reading this."

"Who would want to take the Dare Stone?" Dad asked. "It's not like the thing is worth billions of dollars. Some people still aren't sure it's legit."

Mom shrugged. "Well, it looks like someone wanted it."

Diego lowered his head and stared at his now half-empty plate.

"You wouldn't happen to know anything about this, would you?" Dad joked.

Diego was so despondent he didn't fully catch the joke. "What? What do you mean?"

"Where were you last night, Son? Do you have someone who can verify your whereabouts during the hours this crime happened?"

After his dad pressed the joke harder, Diego caught it and offered a weak smile. "Hilarious. No, I was here all night."

Dad slapped Diego on the back and shook him a little, trying to get him out of his funk. "I know, Son. And look, I know you wanted to go see that exhibit. I do have to say, that stone has been there at Brenau for a long time, most of a century. I find it strange that someone stole it on the very night we were sitting here talking about going to see the thing."

"That *is* weird," Corin added, chiming in for the first time since arriving at the table. "Kind of a creepy coincidence."

"When I woke up this morning," Diego spoke as though he hadn't heard any of the others talking, "I had a feeling something bad happened. At first, I thought I'd just woken up from a strange dream, but then everything seemed normal. I wonder if...if I somehow knew."

"Don't think too much about it, honey," Mom said. "There are bizarre things out there that we don't yet understand. Science is always playing catch up to the universe, and I don't think it ever will, not in our lifetimes and probably beyond. It's possible that our discussion and your focus on this particular piece of history may have bridged some sort of ethereal gap in the quantum reality around us, but it's probably just paranoia. You were so intent on seeing this rock that your mind built up fears around the topic, fears of missing out."

"FOMO," Corin chirped.

The two adults turned their heads toward her and stared with blank expressions.

"Fear of missing out?" Her hands went out as if the answer should have been obvious. "FOMO? You know? It's like a marketing tactic or something. You know how places do the limited-time-only thing for everything from tacos to furniture? Fear of missing out. You don't want to miss the deal."

Then it hit them.

"Right," Mom said, still surprised how much her daughter knew about the subject marketing. "FOMO. Anyway, our minds can sometimes do that to us. They create fears that center around something we desperately desire or find interesting. That's probably all it was."

He appeared to accept the explanation, but in his mind he kept arguing. Mom's thoughts on the matter made complete sense expect for one glaring problem: Why did it all happen on the same night?

It had to be a coincidence—he kept telling himself that—though doing so didn't fix the big issue staring him in the face. He wasn't going to get to see the Dare Stones after all.

Wayne would be disappointed, though that was a small matter. Diego and his friends were in middle school. Surely, the man knew that kids their age couldn't just hop in a car or buy a ticket for a plane to jet around the world and investigate stuff like that on a whim. That was an adult-level freedom.

The thought did give Diego an idea, though; one that pivoted to his original purpose of analyzing the Dare Stones.

His mission materialized in his mind's eye. Now, they had to find the original Dare Stone and take it back to Gainesville. He didn't know how they were going to pull that off, but they had two more weeks before school started to figure it out.

6

CLEMSON, SOUTH CAROLINA

Anton woke, as he always did, at 5:30 in the morning. No matter where he was in the world, or what mission he might have been assigned, his body seemed to sync to that time of day and wake him up. It never failed.

It could be annoying now and then, especially when he wasn't on assignment.

At the moment, however, he *was* on assignment, and so far things were going as planned.

Anton had known that the university would be an easy target, especially for someone as skilled as him. He knew that there would be minimal security, if any, to deal with. While the alarm system at the library was enough to scare away less-capable thieves, it had been a walk in the park for Anton.

He knew that the leaders would be happy with his progress, but he was far from out of the woods yet. Stealing the original Dare Stone was only the first piece to the puzzle.

Anton found it odd that no American research teams or historians had been able to pinpoint the cause of the disappearance of the Lost Colony at Roanoke. He didn't have the answers, either, but he felt like he was every bit as close as anyone had ever come to locating the cause of the colony's disappearance.

That was, after all, his entire purpose for being here.

He sat up in his bed and looked over at his partner, who was still sleeping, breathing heavily after a long night of driving. It had only taken a couple of hours, though to be fair, that drive would have been much shorter had they not taken the precaution of veering off of the main road and using detours just in case they'd been followed.

Gunter would wake up in fifteen, maybe ten minutes. He always slept a little longer than Anton, a fact that made Anton a little jealous from time to time. He wished he could sleep like that, but he knew it was for the best that he couldn't. Anton had always been a light sleeper, always on alert to dangers that were lurking in the shadows.

He'd been that way since before he was recruited by the order.

Anton rested his head against the powder-blue cushion on the headboard and thought back to those days.

He had been a student in one of the best private schools in New England. His parents, wealthy elites from Berlin, had sent him to boarding school in the United States because they said they wanted him to get a good education and be exposed to other cultures, other ways of life.

It didn't take long for Anton to learn the truth.

His parents, it turned out, had sent him there to get him acclimated to American society and culture. They wanted him to be able to blend in anywhere. At first, he didn't know why, but that knowledge came with time.

He had his suspicions, of course, thinking that his mother and father were involved in something either illegal or sketchy, at best. He knew where most of his family money came from. His great-grandfather was Old World money, having built his fortune in weapons manufacturing during the first and second world wars.

And Anton thought it odd that he'd never been taken to see the weapons facilities by his family. After all, if he was going to inherit their financial and business empire, it would make sense that he understood how the business worked, the day-to-day operations, and what they were planning for the future.

Instead, his parents almost seemed to push him away, sending him across the Atlantic to attend a snobby private school in New England.

The school itself was fine, and he found himself making a few friends there with similar backgrounds: rich parents too busy to spend time with their kids or teach them about life, business, and society. It was the same tale again. Wealthy parents were either too involved with their companies or fortunes, or their lifestyles, to spend time raising their kids. In other words, they simply didn't care enough to be real parents.

So, they paid elite private schools to take on the tasks of raising their children.

It was a fact that still stung Anton from time to time, even though he was older and wiser.

Years had passed since those days at the academy. He and his friends had learned much, forged their own way without the guidance of their parents. Still, there'd been an empty hole in Anton. He could see it in some of the other boys, too.

He'd been lucky, though.

During his third year of prep school, he was approached by a stranger, a man who clearly possessed a great amount of money and power.

The man dressed the part of a president or a king and carried himself the same way. There was a sort of regality to him that made him appear to be more important than anyone else in any room he entered.

He never gave Anton his name, not his real one, anyway. That didn't matter. He gave Anton something far more important than a name. He gave him a purpose.

Anton noticed his partner rustling in the bed. Maybe Anton didn't have fifteen more minutes. From the looks of it, Gunter would be up before long, but for now, the man was still snoozing.

The sun still hadn't risen in the east, but a residual glow filtered through the dark sky, signaling that dawn was fast approaching.

Anton had served the organization ever since that day during his junior year in prep school. While he'd told the older man that he needed time to consider the offer, there really wasn't anything to ponder.

The mysterious man left a plain white business card with nothing but a number on it. There was no name, no other identifying information. Simply a number. He'd said all the right things to Anton, making no extraordinary promises but vaguely alluding to a future that was far better than any his parents could ever give him, even with their vast fortune.

At first, Anton wondered why the man had chosen him. Grades alone didn't make someone stand out, nor did test scores. What had it been that this man had seen in Anton to offer him a place at the table, a table where only a select few could sit?

He wasn't sure, but the man had seen something in him, and Anton wasn't about to give up the opportunity of a lifetime. He called the man back that night. Anton's true journey began right then and there.

The older man never gave his last name or even a first name, only a letter, *W*. Anton immediately set about trying to figure out who the stranger was, what his position could be, and why he would have chosen Anton to be a part of his organization. W, however, was a ghost. Anton spent dozens of hours performing online searches but never found a trace of the man, no pictures, no details of any kind.

A person like that was not only powerful but potentially dangerous. That second fact also played a part in Anton's decision to join the organization the man called the Syndicate.

Now, over a decade had passed. Anton was thirty years old.

He'd lived in a castle just outside of the small German city of Wernigerode, where he trained in various forms of hand-to-hand combat, economics, culture, and languages. He'd finished his final two years of school in the United States before returning to Germany, but it was only then he realized how much he truly didn't know.

Once he was initiated into the Syndicate, his eyes were opened.

Gunter tossed in his bed again and rubbed his face. He would be up soon, and it was time to get on the road. The sooner they left the hotel, the better. There wouldn't be many people in the lobby at this time of day, which was good. Few, if any, witnesses would recall seeing the two men. Not that it mattered. They'd been disguised by masks when they robbed the university. No one had any idea who had committed the crime, and Anton was certain the cops had zero leads.

Now that he and Gunter had the Dare Stone in their possession, the real work was about to begin.

His mission was clear: find out what happened to the colony at Roanoke, the source of what drove them mad, and bring it back to W.

When he was given missions, Anton never asked why. He had learned early on that if he were simply to do as instructed his life would be one of luxury and power. Easy enough. His curiosity, however, did needle him in the back of his mind.

It didn't matter. He'd been given enough details. W told him that there was a cause to the madness in Roanoke, something that had driven both the natives in the area and the settlers to insanity.

W suggested it was a device, but what sort was anyone's guess.

Gunter rolled over and propped himself up on a pillow, seeing his partner already awake.

"Time to get going, huh?" Gunter asked in a craggy voice.

Anton nodded. "Yes. We go to the lab and see if there's something to this stone after all."

7

ATLANTA

The kids sat around in Desmond's media room, each staring at a tablet cradled in their hands.

The Ellerbys had purchased the devices for the kids before they went to Italy earlier that summer.

It was much easier for each of them to have their own mini computer than to huddle around Desmond at his desk while he tried to find leads as to the whereabouts of the Dare Stone and the people who took it.

They'd been at it for two hours, scouring the internet, reading news articles, watching video footage, and investigating reports coming in from all over the state and beyond.

Most of what they found wasn't useful, though there were a few interesting tabloid sites that seemed to have their own unique theories on why the stone was taken, who took it, and where it could be.

Corin rubbed her eyes and stood up to stretch, setting the tablet down on the wireless charging station to give it a battery boost before she got back to work. She raised her hands high over her head and leaned to the left, then right. While she stretched, she let out a long exhale.

"Yeah, we've been at this for a bit, huh?" Desmond asked as he, too, stood and stretched. Then he walked over to a small refrigerator next to an auburn-colored couch. He pulled out a bottle of water, twisted off the cap, and took a sip.

Desmond's media room was a glorified playroom. There was a 55-inch high-definition television hanging on the wall, plus the couch, a fridge, two gaming consoles, and his desk in the corner that was home to a MacBook Pro and two additional monitors. There were two black club chairs opposite each other on either side of the couch. Pictures of sports heroes adorned the walls, as did flags from Desmond's favorite teams. There were even a few collectibles from the science fiction movies he loved.

Diego admitted to himself that he'd like to have a room like this someday, but he knew it would be far off in the future since his parents didn't have the same kind of coin as Desmond's.

"We need a new angle," Diego said as he crossed one leg over the other, adjusting his position on the right side of the couch. "We've been using the search engines like a bunch of amateurs."

Desmond chuckled and curled his lips to one side in a curious smirk. "We *are* amateurs. We're in middle school, Bro."

"How do you get to be pro?" Diego countered. "By doing. We have to figure this out another way. I don't think we'll find anything the way we've been doing it."

Corin crossed her arms but remained standing. "What do you have in mind?"

Desmond walked back to the center of the room and sat down in the club chair he'd been using before. "Yeah, I'm all ears if it can save us some time."

"First of all, we're trying to find the people that took the stone, right?" Diego began.

The other two nodded.

"Um, duh?" his sister said.

"Right, but these two guys are clearly pros." He flipped his tablet around and showed the footage he'd been looking at a moment before. "See this?" he said, pointing to the screen.

"It's the security camera from inside the library."

"Yep. Notice anything strange?"

The other two peered closer.

"No, not really?"

Diego sighed. "Watch this closely, and you'll see it."

He hit the play button on the screen, and the others watched with intense focus. It was subtle, so much so that they wouldn't have noticed if Diego hadn't told them to be alert to it. Now, however, it was obvious.

The screenshot was of the part of the library where the entrance to the special collections room was located. The camera monitored that part of the room as well as a huge swath of the main floor of the library. One moment, the library was fine and looking normal.

Then something appeared to slide across the surface of the lens. It wasn't more than a second or two. Then the camera shook a little, as if there was a minor earthquake. It went still again, and the room appeared to be back to normal, although a tad darker than before.

"What was that?" Desmond asked.

"Someone put an image of the library over the camera lens to make it look like no one was there."

Desmond's right eyebrow climbed. "Seems a little low-tech, don't you think?"

"Yes, and I thought the same thing, but you have to keep in mind that the only security they had in this place was an alarm system and a bunch of students who work for campus safety. It's not like they'd have to hack into the system and upload a virus that changed the video stream."

"Fair point. Go on."

"All of this is to say that these two are pros. Even if they used a low-tech method to block the camera view, these are two guys who don't want to be found. From what I've heard and seen online, they may as well be ghosts."

"I don't believe in ghosts," Desmond quipped.

"Me either, but I believe in these two," Diego said as he tapped the screen.

"So," Corin interjected, "if these guys are professionals, adults, and let's assume dangerous, what could the three of us possibly do to find them, stop them, and get the stone back?"

"That's what I was saying. I doubt we could track them down by trying to find their trail, but we already know what they're looking for."

"We do?"

Diego nodded. He tapped one of the tabs on the top of the screen, and a new image came up. It was an article about the Lost Colony of Roanoke, written a few years before.

"They're trying to find the Lost Colony," Diego said, his tone clear and firm.

The other two didn't say anything for a moment—so long, in fact —that Diego wondered if he'd lost them or if they thought he was crazy.

Finally, Desmond broke the silence. "Okay...so, why are these two so interested in the Lost Colony?"

Diego knew that question was going to come up eventually. It was one he'd considered since he first came up with the theory, not that the theory was so out there. It was a pretty obvious conclusion for Diego. And then there was the other problem.

"That's not the only question," Diego said, playing his own opposition. "Why would someone want the stone? There isn't anything inherently valuable about it other than historic, right?"

"Yeah," Corin agreed. "And if the rock had a secret code embedded in the message, surely it would have been deciphered by now."

"Exactly," Diego raised a finger. "That's exactly what I thought."

Desmond's head jerked back and forth in confusion. "So, what are we doing, then? I mean, if they didn't steal the thing for the message, why would they take it? To sell it on the black market?"

"Possibly," Diego admitted. "But I doubt it. I think there must be something else to that stone that no one knows about, or at least hasn't mentioned. Think about it. Sometimes the best place to hide something important is in plain sight."

"Yeah, that's what the guys at IAA say, too," Corin added. "I've heard Mr. Wyatt say that more than once."

Diego nodded in agreement. "So, even if there was something more to the stone, no one would know about it, and no one would suspect because it was put on display in a minimum-security college library."

"Okay," Desmond said, cutting his friend off. "That's all great, but it still doesn't explain to us what the thing really is and why the two men who stole it are looking for the Lost Colony."

"You've read the translations," Diego said.

"Yeah, a dozen times already."

"Yep. And surely, those two would have seen the translations, too."

"Hence why they wouldn't need to steal the thing. They could just look it up online," Corin pointed out.

"Right. So, I wonder if they believe the stone has some kind of scientific property to it that they think will lead them to the Lost Colony."

"Scientific property? You mean like magnetic or something?"

"Could be," Diego shrugged. "I have no idea. But if they're looking for the Lost Colony, we know they'll likely be heading toward North Carolina, probably the coast where Roanoke was established in the 1500s."

Desmond sighed and shook his head. "Even if that's the case, it's not a small area. Those guys could be anywhere between Gainesville and the Outer Banks. We'll never find them."

"Not to mention," Corin added, "we're just kids. What could we possibly do against a couple of professionals? That's assuming there are only two of them."

Diego knew they were right. He'd considered their points before the other two uttered the words.

"You're both right. I know. These guys are clearly experts, way more than the two we took down in Italy."

The others confirmed this with a nod, but he didn't stop.

"And you're right about us not being able to find them without some kind of help. We'd need someone with technology, tracking systems, and connections all over the South, maybe even the world. Stuff that three middle school kids like us don't have."

"Why do I feel like you're agreeing with us but also not really agreeing with us?" Corin asked.

Diego's eyes narrowed, and his lips twitched, almost stretching to a grin. "Because...I know someone who might be able to help us with all that?"

"The cops?" Desmond asked. "Because it sounds like something the cops should handle. Or maybe the FBI. They're probably already in on the investigation."

"Maybe they are. Maybe the cops are working around the clock to find the guys who did this. As of this moment, though, I doubt they have much of a head start on us. It's worth a shot, guys. This is what we do, right? Are we the Adventure Guild, or are we just three kids who did that thing one time in Italy? This is what we were born to do. And I'm going to keep trying to figure this out, with or without you."

He turned and started for the door. He was nearly to it when Corin stopped him.

"Diego? Wait."

He paused for a second and then slowly spun around to face her. She was standing with her arms crossed, a determined gaze in her eyes. "What's your plan?"

8

ATLANTA

The three kids stared with pleading eyes at the man in the chair. If they could have added sparkling lights to make their pupils twinkle, they would have. From the look on the man's face, he wasn't giving in to their request.

"No," he said plainly.

"Aww, come on, Sam. We just need you to take us into the city for an hour or so." Desmond's begging was on point. He'd clearly done this dance with Sam before.

Sam Tuttle was the head of security for the Ellerbys. He went with them on international and domestic trips that involved treasure hunts, searches for artifacts, and speaking engagements. He was also invited on vacations so he could get a little rest and relaxation, but Sam never seemed to shut off the bodyguard role. He was always on high alert.

"No, but thanks for asking. Now, if you two don't mind, I am going golfing this afternoon, and I really need to work on my 4-iron. It's gotten a tad loose since I last played."

Desmond's frown furrowed. "You play golf?"

"You know I do, Dez. Seriously, get your parents to take you to downtown. I'm sure they'd be happy to."

"They're busy. You know that. Come on, Sam. Please. I won't bother you for anything else for...a month?"

Sam snorted so hard he had to wipe his nose. "Come on, Dez. You always ask me for help with stuff like this. I'm basically your chauffeur half the time."

"So, you'll do it?"

"Absolutely not." He stood up and made his way toward the door.

"Seriously? What do you have going on tomorrow that's so pressing that you can't take a little drive downtown with us?"

Sam froze and took a deep breath. Then he exhaled slowly and twisted around. "I have a date tomorrow night, okay? Happy now?"

The three kids all raised their eyebrows at this new revelation.

"Uh...a date?" Desmond asked.

"With a girl?" Corin added.

Sam's head bounced from one to the other. "Yes. With a girl...a woman, actually," he corrected. "I'm taking her out for a nice dinner."

"Where you taking her?" Diego pressed, knowing that Downtown Atlanta and Buckhead were secretly treasure troves of international cuisine. Atlanta's food scene was one of the best kept secrets in the world. It was an international city in every sense of the word and boasted restaurants that brought influences from every corner of the planet.

Sam sighed. "Marcel. Okay. I'm taking her to Marcel."

Desmond's eyes widened. "You must like her. Marcel over in the West End district?"

"Yes. Now, if you're done with your inquisition, I need to get going."

"To the driving range?"

"Yes. Goodbye, Desmond and you two." He waved a hand and started to turn back to the door.

"What time is your reservation?" Desmond asked.

Another exaggerated exhale escaped the bodyguard's lips. "Seven. Okay?"

"Perfect," Desmond exclaimed. "You can run us over to the IAA building in the morning and be back before lunch. No big deal."

Sam didn't respond, apparently considering the request. At least that's what the three kids hoped. "Why do you need to go to the IAA building?" Suspicion laced his words.

"We need to ask Tara and Alex some questions," Diego offered.

"Questions?"

The three nodded.

"Yes, about some stuff we're researching."

"Is this *stuff* going to get you into more trouble like it did in Italy? Because, frankly, I don't feel much like going through that again."

"I hope not," Desmond said. "We just want to ask them about what happened at Brenau with the Dare Stone. We want to know more about all that."

"I knew it." Sam fully turned and jabbed a finger at the three kids. "I knew you were going to get into something that involved some kind of trouble or something dangerous."

"It's not dangerous," Corin argued. "We just want to know more about those stones and why someone would take one." It was sort of true.

"Come on, Sam," Desmond pushed. "It's like twenty minutes to get over to the IAA building. It's not like we're asking you to drive us three hours away or anything like that."

Sam drew in a deep breath and exhaled. "Fine. I'll take you, but if at any moment this little babysitting trip turns south, I'm bringing you back home."

"Understood. Well, except I don't like you calling it a babysitting trip."

"I don't care. That's what it feels like I'm doing."

"Fair enough."

"And another thing."

The three kids waited to hear what the next condition would be. They had a bad feeling it was going to be something that would cramp their style.

"You stay in my sight the entire time. That means you don't leave my side from the second we get out of the car until the moment we walk back into this house. Do I make myself clear?" Sam's stern tone matched the look on his face. It was an expression that told Desmond and the others that there would be no bending on this one. The bodyguard wanted total obedience and adherence to his request. If they didn't agree or didn't do what he said, then Sam would probably never give them a chance to do something like this again.

"Fine," Desmond relented. "We won't wander off."

"That's...actually a better way of putting it," Sam confessed sheepishly. Then he cracked a grin. "Okay. Get your things. I'll get the car and bring it around."

Desmond's face scrunched in confusion. "What do you mean? I thought you were going to the driving range or something."

"It's not like going to the range is going to help my game. And not going isn't going to hurt it. I don't get to play enough to make a difference, anyway. Besides, I'm not taking you to the IAA building tomorrow. I'm keeping my entire day clear so that I don't screw up that date."

"Sounds like you really like this girl," Corin chirped, elongating the word *really*.

Her suspicion was confirmed when his face reddened, the cheeks turning a bright pink. It was a reaction they'd never seen out of the hardened security man before.

"Okay, okay. Get your stuff. Unless you three don't want to go to the IAA building. In which case, I will hit the driving range."

"No, no!" Diego cut in. "We'll get ready. Today is perfect."

"You did call ahead, right? You know, to let Tara and Alex know you're coming?"

Desmond and the others exchanged a bewildered glance.

Sam sighed again. "Fine. I'll call and make sure they're in the building."

"From what I hear, they never leave," Corin offered.

"They gotta sleep somewhere and sometime."

He pulled out his phone and started searching through his contacts for the IAA headquarters in Downtown Atlanta. Then he noticed the three kids were still just watching him.

"Hey, I thought I asked you to get ready. I'm calling them. I'll bring the car around in a minute."

"Right," Desmond said. Then the three set in motion, grabbing their tablets and book bags, put on their shoes, and scooped up some extra bottles of water for the visit to the IAA.

9

GREENVILLE, SOUTH CAROLINA

Gunter peeled open the corrugated metal door and allowed his partner to pass through first. Once Anton was inside the warehouse, Gunter took a quick look around to make sure they hadn't been followed. He knew as well as anyone that just because the gravel parking lot was empty didn't mean they weren't being watched. Vigilance was the ultimate guiding principle in their line of work.

He stepped inside and pulled the door closed, sliding a heavy steel bolt through a receiver above the handle and a second below it.

The inside of the warehouse was dark and dusty. Rusted girders ran along the ceiling amid patches where the metal roofing had given way to time and weather, allowing oxidized gaps to open in the weakest points. The holes in the roof provided the only light in the derelict building, and the sun's rays shone through as though they were dim lasers from the heavens.

Anton walked steadily toward the office attached to the left side of the warehouse interior. In its prime, this building had been a place of production. Forty years before, forklifts and carts would have been everywhere, rushing to transport their loads to trailers at the loading docks. Men and women would have been toiling away, lifting heavy boxes or documenting the payload for each transport vehicle coming and going.

Now, though, it was a shell of its former self.

There were many such buildings in similar swaths across the nation. Cities that had relied on the Industrial Age to build their wealth had faded with the onset of modern technology such as automation and the cheaper labor that American companies sought overseas. Relics such as this were no longer useful, mostly due to the fact that they weren't in a prime location for logistical efficiency. Most of the major corporations owned their own warehouses and built them close to larger cities or hubs. That left places like this one with almost no purpose, except for now.

Anton's organization had purchased the building for pennies on the dollar. The seller had been happy to rid himself of it, and the organization needed a base of operations in the Southeast that could allow for ease of movement throughout the region. They also purchased an older brick building in Chattanooga, Tennessee, a few hours to the west. That one was an old saddlery that had long since ceased operations, its cause of death identical to that of the warehouse.

The order owned condemned and abandoned buildings all throughout the Southeast and were expanding westward with every passing month. For now, they were nothing more than safe houses, places where operatives like Anton and Gunter could go to escape pursuit or where they could seek shelter in case of emergencies.

In this instance, the warehouse was one of the best research facilities the order owned. While on the outside it looked like nothing but a rundown old foundry, the inside held a secret no one, not even stray citizens, would find.

Anton pushed open the metal door to the office. The hinges protested with a loud, squeaky groan. He stepped inside and around behind an old desk that looked like it was left over from the 1960s. The thing had a Formica top that was peeling at the corners. The legs and body were metal and painted a sort of seafoam-green color, though it was difficult to tell what the faded paint might have originally looked like.

Gunter closed the door tight behind him and stepped closer to the desk as Anton reached under it and pressed his finger to a scanning switch invisible to the untrained eye. The device scanned his fingerprint, and then a click came from behind him.

The back wall suddenly creaked and then began sliding backward, the bottom edge grinding on the hard concrete floor. When it stopped moving, the wall had revealed a secret stairwell to the right set into the wall. Lights flickered on in the hidden corridor as the two men made their way down the steps.

When they reached the bottom, they entered a room that was designed more like a bunker. They were surrounded on all sides by thick concrete walls. A steel table sat in the middle, and there were four black leather chairs surrounding it. Computers rested atop counters running down every side of the room except the one with the only door in and out.

Among the computers were several other pieces of equipment—microscopes, sensors, and testing equipment hooked up to some of the computers for analysis. All of it revealed the real nature of the space. This place was a laboratory, one of the only ones of its kind that the organization owned in this part of the country. The next closest one was in Atlanta, but there was no way the two men were going to stick around there. Too many eyeballs and too many cops, not to mention the traffic.

Anton placed the stone on the steel table under the lights, while Gunter picked up a pair of safety glasses from a rack near the door. He put on a pair of white gloves and then strode over to the wall on the left where a series of tools were kept in black metal drawers and a shelf that ran up to the ceiling. Gunter took a miniature drill out of the second drawer and returned to the table where Anton had been busily securing the stone with a set of cushioned Vise Grips.

The two men clearly knew what they were doing. They'd performed this exact task a couple of other times in other labs. Now it was old hat to them. They fell into their rhythm, one monitoring the rock while the other drilled into it. Gunter guided the drill expertly, making sure that he didn't break off the bit, which he'd done dozens of times while training for this operation. Now, he was surgical with the tool.

The hollow drill bit bore into the hard rock, carving out a cylindrical piece of the stone. When he was satisfied he'd gone deep enough, Gunter gently withdrew the tool, careful to pull it straight out from the rock's surface so the sample wouldn't be damaged.

Then, when the bit was completely removed, he set the tool on the edge of the table and helped Anton unclamp the Vise Grips from the edges of the rock.

Ever so cautiously, Anton raised the stone with his gloved hands and tilted it over, allowing the new sample to slide out onto a white cloth he'd placed on the table. The tiny tube fell out and onto the makeshift cushion. The piece of rock was little more than a sliver, but it was all the two men needed to make sure the stone they'd stolen from the university was what they'd hoped.

Gunter picked up the sample with a pair of tweezers and placed it into a glass dish then walked over to a machine that looked like a glass box with metal corners. The device was connected to the nearest computer, and while he set about placing the sample inside the machine, Anton fired up the desktop and prepared the necessary software for their test.

It took the two men five minutes before everything was ready to go. When Gunter gave the thumbs-up, Anton entered the commands into the computer, and the machine came to life.

It glowed a bright white light as it ran through the process of analyzing the sample. The process took less than a minute. Then the bright lights faded, and the computer screen began populating with spectral images of the sample, as well as with data related to what the stone sample contained at the elemental and molecular levels.

As the seconds ticked by, Anton's face strained as the signals he expected to see as a result of the test never came. There were no anomalies in this sample, no analytical code on the monitor that would confirm the presence of quantium in the rock.

"What's the problem?" Gunter asked in their native German, also confused by the absence of the desired element.

"I'm not sure," Anton answered. "You extracted the core sample correctly."

"Perhaps we need to try a different section of the rock."

Anton thought for a moment, and then looked over his shoulder at the stone resting on the table. He and his partner had gone through this process before, and they weren't given to mistakes. Something was wrong, though, and he wasn't sure what it could be.

He turned back to the monitor and scrolled back to the top of the list of elements on the screen. As he read through the list, the look of concern on his face dug deep lines across his forehead and stretched from the corners of his eyes.

"Something is wrong," he said.

He stood up straight and stepped over to the table where the stone still sat. He picked it up with both hands and held it close to his face as he peered at the surface, as if his naked eyes could detect the issue that modern technology could not. Anton drew in a deep breath and then abruptly smashed the breadth of the stone against the table.

The hard metal reverberated and sent a loud clank through the room that hurt both men's ears. The force of the blow was enough, though, and the rock split in two. At first, Gunter stared in horror at his partner. The man had just sealed his fate with the head of the order. Their leader would not be happy about this. He'd been clear what would happen to any of his operatives who failed. This was beyond a failure. It was blatant disobedience. They'd been tasked with securing artifacts that were known, or believed, to contain quantium and keep those artifacts in their original condition so that the element could be extracted at their facilities in Europe.

Now, this artifact was broken.

Gunter swallowed hard, realizing that his fate would likely be tied directly to Anton's.

"What have you done?" Gunter asked in a horrified voice. Visions of running from the order were already flashing through his mind, even though he knew there was nowhere he could go that they couldn't find him. Their resources were infinite, and there was no place to hide.

The dust settled from Anton's rash action, and he looked over at his partner, holding up the two sections of the rock. On the outside, the stone looked ancient; signs of weathering and age were evident, lending the exterior credibility as legitimate. The inside, however, was gray and crumbling, the obvious signs of something manufactured by man.

The look in Gunter's eyes showed he immediately understood, though he was still confused as to how they'd been duped.

Anton looked down at the cut sections of rock, and then his head raised slowly to meet Gunter's befuddled gaze. "It's a fake."

10

ATLANTA

The three kids and their chaperone walked through the glass doors of the International Archaeological Agency and stepped into the lobby. The shiny white marble floor was dotted with contrasting glossy black tiles that reflected the LED lights hanging from long cables above.

The reception desk to the right was occupied by a petite redheaded woman. An older black man with streaks of black in a white beard stood next to her in a security guard uniform.

The two smiled at the group as they approached.

Desmond and the two siblings spun around in circles, taking in the huge room with wide eyes. There were pictures of artifacts the agency had recovered hanging on the walls in massive glass display frames that were bolted to the walls with silver pegs. The high ceiling appeared to stretch four floors up to where a walkway circled the top floor, protected by a brushed steel rail.

"This place is so awesome," Desmond muttered under his breath.

"Yes, it is," Diego agreed.

"Hello there," the receptionist greeted them. "You must be the ones here to see Alex and Tara, right?"

The kids nodded eagerly. They'd met the two young lab assistants before at an event the Ellerbys held just ten days before, only a couple of days after arriving back from Italy. Now, here they were in the headquarters of one of the most important historical salvage operations in the world.

Tara and Alex were frequently referred to as "the kids," but now that there were actual kids in the building, the receptionist had to alter her references. She stood up and walked around the desk, leaving the grinning security guard standing next to it.

"Mind manning the phone for me while I show them down to the lab?"

"Not at all, Lizzy. Y'all have fun down in the lab."

"We will," Corin said with a smile that mirrored his.

Sam simply gave the man a polite nod, as though there were some secret security guy language that they both spoke without using words.

The four visitors followed Lizzy to a door in the back corner of the room. She held up her security badge to a keypad and waited until the thing beeped. Then she spoke into a hidden microphone, giving her full name. "Elisabeth Harkins."

Something buzzed inside the door, and then it clicked before swinging open.

Lizzy turned to the four guests and motioned them through. "This way."

They stepped into a corridor with gray walls and a white tile floor. Lizzy led them down to the end of the hall, where an elevator with steel doors waited. She pressed the down arrow, and the doors opened immediately.

The doors closed, and when they reopened, the visitors were greeted by a long wall of glass to their left framed by black aluminum. Through the glass, they could see the vast laboratory that was the working home of Tara and Alex.

The young married couple was in the middle of the room, their hands clad in white gloves. They wore white surgical masks and appeared to be brushing an old rock with brushes much like the ones the kids had seen on archaeological digs. While Corin and Diego hadn't spent as much time on dig sites as their friend Desmond, they'd seen the tools frequently on television shows and once or twice in person when their parents took them to a local dig.

The visitors stood at the door and waited until the two researchers noticed them. Alex looked up and waved the group in. Lizzy acknowledged with a nod and waved her badge in front of a similar card reader as the one in the lobby. Then she leaned down and looked into a glass pane fixed into the panel. A red line crossed her face, and then a voice said, "Welcome, Elisabeth."

The door opened, and she stepped inside, but the kids lingered with mouths agape. They stared at the high-tech security panel in rapt wonder.

"Are you coming?" Lizzy asked with a grin.

The kids answered by nodding absently, but they were still gazing at the access panel.

"I've only seen those in the movies," Desmond said.

Lizzy's pleasant expression never changed. "Yes, these are state of the art. Though this kind of tech has been around a long time, we just made the upgrade after recent...events."

She let the conversation die as they passed through a metal archway and into the lab.

A slight tingle washed over the group, and the kids looked around, as if wondering who'd touched them or what had happened.

"Ionic air static stabilization," she said, sensing their confusion. "It's like a clean room without the room. Takes away any static you may have brought in with your clothes." She paused and leaned close to the kids' faces. "That one," she whispered, "is our own invention."

She straightened up and turned toward Tara and Alex, who were busy removing their gloves and masks.

"I brought you some visitors," Lizzy said proudly. She turned back to the kids. "Have a good time, you three. And you, too," she flashed a grin at Sam. He blushed and nodded respectfully at her.

Lizzy brushed past him as she sauntered toward the exit, the scent of her flowery perfume washing over him in her wake.

He snapped his head to reset his senses as the two researchers approached them.

"Welcome, gang. How are you guys today?" Tara asked.

"Good," the kids took turns answering.

"I'm Sam Tuttle." The bodyguard extended his hand to Tara. She shook it and nodded, then he shook Alex's hand before taking a step back. "Nice place you got here."

"Thanks," Alex said. "It's our personal playground."

"I'll say," Diego chimed, momentarily sounding like a kid from the 1950s.

"We enjoy our work. That's for sure."

The kids' heads were spinning as they twisted around, scouring their surroundings and taking in every detail. There were fragments of ancient Greek pottery; a *gladius*, or sword, from ancient Rome; and papyrus stretched out on a worktable and covered in a huge sheet of glass that pressed down the old paper. Upon closer inspection, they could see that the glass was actually a case of its own and locked the papyrus in an airtight seal.

"Pretty cool, huh?" Alex said.

"Yes. Very cool," Desmond answered.

"So," Tara said, clapping her hands together once, shaking her dark auburn hair that dangled just below her ears. "Sam called us and said you three had some questions you wanted to ask?"

"Yes, ma'am," Diego spoke up. "We were wondering about the theft at Brenau University. We were hoping you could help us figure out what happened."

"To the Dare Stone?" Alex asked, surprisingly chipper about the subject.

"Yes, sir."

Alex chortled and shook his head. "You don't have to call me sir."

"And the ma'am thing can be dropped, too," Tara added.

"Sorry. It's how we were raised. I know you two aren't old, but we were taught to be polite to everyone, not just older people but younger, too."

Tara and Alex shared a beaming glance.

"Well, we appreciate that, but you can lose the formality here with us. It's great to see some parents are still teaching their kids the respectful way to engage with others."

"So, what would you like to know about the incident at Brenau?" Alex asked.

"You mean the stone," Sam corrected. "They want to know about the stone."

"Um...yes, the stone," Desmond said. "We were wondering what you know about it."

The married couple glanced at each other again, this time sharing an unspoken knowledge.

"What?" Corin pressed. "What was that look for?"

Tara and Alex faced the visitors, both crossing their arms.

"We can tell you, but we'd have to eliminate you," Tara said menacingly.

The kids took a step back as one.

"I'm just kidding," Tara added quickly. "But we do need you to keep it a secret."

"Can you keep secrets?" Alex asked.

The three all nodded eagerly.

Tara cocked her head to the side as if contemplating whether or not to believe the kids. "I don't know, Alex. What do you think?"

He wrinkled his nose and flattened his lips into a stoic frown. "Well, I guess we can tell them. They're friends with the boss man, after all."

"That's true." She grinned broadly. "Come over here and have a look at this."

She motioned toward the table where she and Alex had been brushing a piece of rock when the group arrived.

They stopped at the table and looked to the middle where a white cloth was piled on top of the stone.

"What do you know about the Chowan River Stone or the original Dare Stone?" Alex asked when everyone was gathered around the table.

Desmond swallowed, unwilling to answer. He felt like he was

standing with a couple of his heroes. Everyone knew who the IAA was. They were world-famous artifact hunters, and these two were the brains and tech behind every expedition. Even the Ellerbys, who were well known in the archaeology community in their own right, looked up to the IAA and their work.

"You mean, like where it was found?" Diego asked. "North Carolina, by a man named Louis Hammond. He went by L.E. Hammond. He was from California and touring the country when he stopped for a break and stumbled on to the stone."

"That's correct," Tara pointed out, "but that's not what I meant. Clearly, you were aware that the stone was at Brenau in their library."

The kids nodded.

"Well, that isn't entirely true." There was a hint of mischief in her voice, and her crooked smile only served to emphasize that.

"What do you mean, entirely true?" Corin asked.

Alex chuckled and then reached across the table. He plucked the cloth from the stone, revealing it in its entirety.

"Wait a second. That can't be," Diego protested. "That's not possible. Two men took that last night."

"Did they?" Alex asked with raised eyebrows.

There on the table in the lab of the IAA was the infamous Chowan River Stone.

11

ATLANTA

"How do you have that?" Corin demanded, a little louder than intended. She immediately apologized for the escalation of her voice.

"It's okay," Alex reassured her. "I get it. You've obviously heard what happened last night at Brenau."

"Uh, yeah."

"Well, the truth is that we borrowed the stone from Brenau about two weeks ago."

"Borrowed?" Desmond asked.

"Yes. We got permission from the university to bring the real stone here. The one that was stolen last night was a forgery, a fake, one that we created here in our lab."

The kids were stunned, and their faces showed it.

"Wait a second," Diego stopped them. "You're telling us that the stone those two crooks took last night wasn't the real Dare Stone, the original one?"

"That's exactly what we're telling you," Tara confirmed. "A friend tipped us off that there were two guys in the area, red-flag guys. We tracked them to Gainesville. When they showed up on security cameras having a casual look at the stone, we knew what their target would be."

"Target? Red-flag guys?" Sam's voice was full of bewilderment. "What is going on here?"

Alex nodded. "Probably best we start from the beginning. We can take a look at the stone in a minute. Come on. Have a seat." He motioned to several chairs at the next table over, and the group maneuvered around the displays and worktables to get a seat close to the two researchers.

When everyone was seated, Alex returned with a laptop and set it on the table in front of the last empty chair. He spun the monitor around so the guests could see it. There was a black-and-white image of the special collections room at the Brenau University library.

"See the two guys in the picture?"

The visitors leaned closer and peered at the image.

"One in the top-right corner," Corin said. "He's pretending to examine one of the other stones while the second guy is standing there in the middle looking at a different stone."

Tara and Alex exchanged a curious glance.

"Very good. And why do you think that one in the top of the picture is pretending?" Tara asked.

"Because of the way his head is tilted. It looks like maybe he's keeping an eye on his partner, or possibly the rest of the room. Either way, he's clearly not interested in the stone in front of him."

Tara nodded with pride. "I'm impressed," she said. "I dare say most cops wouldn't see that. It's usually a pretty trained eye to spot something that obscure."

Corin blushed at the compliment.

"But you're correct. These two are working together. The rest of the people in the image are just visitors."

"The men," Alex interjected, "are Anton Schneider and Gunter Becker. "They've been at the scene of at least three other thefts like this one in the last two months. Every time, between a week to two weeks before the heist happens."

Sam listened closely, but things had quickly spiraled into his element, and he couldn't keep quiet any longer. "You've been tracking them, huh?"

"Not just us," Tara confessed. "Interpol, FBI, MI5. All of them have been following these two."

"So...I hate to ask the obvious question, but why didn't you stop them from taking the...what's it called?"

"Dare Stone," Diego informed.

"Right. The Dare Stone."

"They dropped off the map about three weeks ago, but we had a tip that they were looking into the stones—the Chowan River Stone, to be precise. The others are pretty useless."

"And worthless," Alex added.

"Yes."

"I'm sorry," Sam interrupted. "You said you had a tip they were looking into the stones?"

"That's correct," Tara said. "We were aware of this because they weren't very coy about their questions when they showed up in the area about three weeks ago. A couple of German guys walking around in eastern Georgia and western North Carolina tend to get noticed. We managed to convince the university to let us take the original stone and replace it with a replica. Since it's in a glass case, no ordinary visitors would be able to tell the difference."

"So, you set a trap?" Sam asked.

"Yes. We worked with the FBI and Interpol on that. We replaced the stone with the fake and brought it here under close watch. We've been analyzing it for the last several days. It's a remarkable piece."

"I'm sorry, but you let the thieves go. They could be anywhere."

"Oh, we're not worried," Tara said. "The FBI followed them north to Dahlonega. The men holed up for the night there in a hotel. The feds have been watching them since they arrived, hoping to get information about who they work for and what they're doing."

"You think this is bigger than just a simple heist?" Diego asked, realizing it was probably the first time in his life he'd used the word *heist*.

"We do," Alex said. "Well, we do now. We didn't know about any of this until last month when the FBI reached out. Tommy put us on it."

The kids nodded their understanding.

"So, the feds are tapping those two to find out who they work for, who their buyer is, that sort of thing?"

Tara and Alex shared another look, though this one was fraught with trepidation, as if they were holding something back from their guests.

Tara was the first to nod. "It's okay. We know them. And the boss trusts them."

"Okay," Alex rolled his shoulders. "Come over here."

He motioned to a desk against the far wall. There was a strange machine on one end of it that looked like a small encased 3-D printer. It was apparent the device wasn't that. There were metal tubes going into the top and sides. Within the case, a platform was held up in the center by two black rods. Two more rods protruded into the middle, each with a matching nob on the ends. The machine was connected to another computer to the right. The black computer tower displayed green LED lights from the front and two grooves on the side.

"Did you build this computer?" Corin asked as the group stopped at the table.

"Sure did," Tara said. "We build most of our tech here, even manu-factured our own quantum chips."

"Quantum chips? As in quantum computers?"

Tara smiled proudly. "Yep."

"These computers are far more powerful than anything else on the market right now," Alex said. "This box thingy here," he pointed at the case, "analyzes materials and feeds the information into the computer. We control the outputs and inputs from the desktop as well."

"Awesome," Desmond whispered reverently.

"For sure," Diego agreed.

"Yeah, it's pretty cool." Alex shifted over to the mouse and clicked it once. The screen bloomed to life and displayed something that looked like a cylinder on the screen.

"What is that?" Diego asked.

"That, my friend, is a sample from the original Dare Stone. We used a micro drill to get into the core of the rock. The drill is so small, no one at Brenau will notice when we return it to their library—after they make some security changes, of course."

"You drilled into the Dare Stone?" Diego sounded a little incensed.

"Yes, but we had to."

"Why?" Corin asked. "It's just a rock."

Tara shook her head. "That's what we thought, too, but we went on a hunch, one that we knew the FBI, MI5, and Interpol would have never considered."

"Which was?"

Alex clicked the mouse again, and the screen changed to a recent news article about a necklace that had been taken from the British Museum. "MI5 is on board with this investigation because of this theft. The two men who took the fake stone from Brenau are the same ones who stole this necklace in the UK. They also broke into a church in Germany and stole a bracelet three weeks before that."

"What kind of bracelet?" Desmond asked. "And what was so special about that necklace?"

Alex narrowed his eyes as he grinned. "Nothing gets by you three. I like that. There was nothing special about the pieces that were taken, other than that they were old and historically significant. Which, to us, is enough, but to a criminal looking to make some money, those two items won't fetch much."

"It's their simplicity that hides what we believe to be what is truly valuable about those objects."

"What do you mean?"

"Watch," Alex answered. He clicked the mouse, and a new window opened.

This one contained a video feed from what appeared to be a surveillance camera. There were display cases all around the room and against the walls. Each held different items from long ago.

Alex hit the play button, and the video began. "This is the night the necklace was taken. Pay close attention to the emergency lights in the top corner of the room."

After ten seconds, two figures appeared in the scene. They went straight for a display case near the corner. One of the masked men attached a small metal disc to the glass and stepped back. In seconds, the glass exploded into a thousand pieces. The emergency lights in the corner flashed on, but when the second thief picked up the necklace, he did something strange. He held it up to the lights. Suddenly, the floodlights flickered and then exploded, casting the room into darkness.

Corin's breath caught. The two boys shuddered at the abrupt and bizarre occurrence, nearly taking a step back at the sight.

The video stopped playing, and Alex looked at his guests with a blank expression. Then he clicked the mouse again, and the screen returned to the image of the cylinder from before.

"What was that?" Desmond stuttered.

Alex and Tara grinned at their guests. It was an expression that told the three visitors both hosts shared the same answer.

"That, my young friends," Tara said, "was quantium."

12

GREENVILLE

"How is it a fake?" Gunter asked, his voice rising with frustration. "I thought the rest of the stones were fake. This one was supposed to be real."

"I know," Anton said, putting his hands up in an equal display of irritation. "I don't understand what happened."

Gunter thumbed his jaw for a moment, cradling his chin in his forefinger. His cold, icy blue eyes peered at the two halves of stone as he contemplated their quandary. He ran his other hand through his short blond hair and then dropped both hands to his sides.

"What do we tell the boss?" he asked.

His question was legitimate enough but one that Anton wasn't going to entertain, not the way Gunter anticipated, anyway.

"We're not going to tell the boss anything," Anton answered.

"He's going to demand an update within the next twenty-four hours. Maybe sooner. You know this."

"I'm aware of what his expectations are, Gunter. But you know as well as I do what will happen if we tell him the stone we stole was the wrong one, that it was a fake. You know what he does to those who fail him."

Gunter swallowed hard. He was a tough guy, one who'd been

through rigorous military training. And that had been just the beginning. After his stint with the German army, he'd been recruited by the order to work for them in a more clandestine role. He would operate as a ghost, sometimes on military-style operations, sometimes committing what more closely aligned to what most would consider criminal activity, such as the theft of the Dare Stone. Through it all, he'd remained stoic, unafraid of anything. Almost anything.

Their leader, a man whose name remained a mystery to everyone who worked under him, was not a man of mercy. Failure was dealt with swiftly. It was those dealings that Gunter sought to avoid, and he knew that his partner sought the same.

"What do you suggest, then?" Gunter asked. "If we're not going to tell him, are you saying we lie to him? Tell him that the rock was never real to begin with?" He motioned to the broken stone.

"No," Anton said, jerking his head to the side. "We know that Brenau had an artifact that contained quantium. Our scans a few weeks ago confirmed it. And we isolated it to that rock," he jammed his index finger at the stone.

"True. So, what are you saying?"

"I'm saying we were duped. Someone must have changed out the stone with a replica."

Gunter's eyelids narrowed as he considered the possibility. "So, they knew we were coming? How? Did someone sell us out?"

Anton shook off the notion. "I doubt that. We were careful. We're always careful."

"Not careful enough, apparently."

"No, we were. Something happened, though." He paced to the opposite wall and put his hands on his hips, staring at the shelf of tools. "I doubt anyone spotted us, though it would be foolish for us to discount that entirely."

"Maybe the university took the real stone to another lab to run some tests. They do that sort of thing all the time with their archaeology students. While they were studying the stone, it could be that their standard procedure is to replace it with a replica temporarily so visitors can feel like they're still seeing the authentic artifact."

It was a good explanation and certainly made more sense than either of the two men somehow blowing their cover. They'd been careful, hadn't they?

Anything was possible, and Anton knew that they certainly weren't without flaw. If someone had been watching them—or at the very least had been aware of their presence—when they were doing recon at the university, it was not outside the realm of possibility that the authorities in charge of the college could have pulled the real stone and replaced it with the fake.

"We need to find out what they did with the real stone," he said.

Gunter looked incredulous. "How are we going to do that? I hope you're not suggesting we go back to Gainesville. They'll be watching for us there now."

"No," Anton agreed. "I don't think that would be wise. We can figure out what happened to the real stone without taking such drastic measures."

Suddenly, the phone in his pocket beeped three times. The two men looked up at each other with concern filling their eyes.

It was an alarm Anton had connected to his phone. Someone had tripped a laser at one of the entrances to the building.

He immediately shifted over to one of the computers, clicked the mouse, and pulled up the security video feed.

Gunter stepped over to the door and pressed a red button next to the frame. A deep grinding sound resonated from the ceiling and the stairwell as the secret door started sliding shut again.

Anton watched the monitor closely as the federal agents swarmed the perimeter of the building and closed in on the front and rear doors. Most of them donned navy-blue vests with the yellow letters *FBI* on them. Others were in black windbreakers, police uniforms, or street clothes. Several wore SWAT gear and led the charge toward the building.

"I count two dozen," Anton said. "Split evenly in the front and back. Plus there are several more waiting, probably as reinforcements or to corral us on the property, block off our escape."

Gunter turned and strode back to the door. There wasn't an ounce of concern on his face now. Anton's expression also lacked any semblance of worry. To a casual observer, they might wonder how the men were remaining so calm in the face of such incredible odds. Not these two. If an observer didn't know any better, they'd swear they were the ones outnumbering the enemy.

Spinning on his heels, Gunter rounded the table and made his way to the back corner of the room, where several black cases were lined up and stacked two or three high. He grabbed one of the hard-shell cases from the top and spun around, setting it on top of the table. Then he pulled down another and placed it next to the first. He opened both cases, revealing white FPV headsets and radios. Gunter set one pair on the table for Anton and took the other headset out and fit it over his head just above his eyes. He picked up the controller that was bound to the receiver and flipped the power switch and then the arming switch. Then he pulled the headset down over his eyes and waited.

Anton stepped over to the table and went through the same process until the camera attached to his drone blinked to life.

"Ready?" he asked.

"When you are," Gunter responded.

"Go."

Anton's drone lifted from its charging station atop a concrete column in the corner of the warehouse. He could see his partner's drone doing the same in the opposite corner of the building. The picture was incredibly clear for a radio transmission, thanks to some high-end transmitters.

The feds and their support teams surrounded the doors, unaware of the danger lurking inside.

One of the men thought he heard something and turned to his superior before trying to open the door. "You hear that?" he asked.

The guy in charge, wearing a navy-blue windbreaker with bright maize letters on it nodded. "Take it down."

The first man nodded and pulled on the door. It was locked, as he suspected, but they were prepared for such a contingency. They'd already attached plastic explosives around the frame. The team on the other side of the building had done the same, also anticipating a similar obstacle.

In most cases, they would use a battering ram to knock down a door, but this entrance was different than others. While using small explosives might hurt someone on the inside, that was their own fault. They should have opened the door when they had the chance, not that the feds had given that kind of choice. This wasn't a warrant service. This was a raid, plain and simple.

They'd tracked the two thieves to his warehouse, all the way from Gainesville and Dahlonega. Now, the two men were trapped, and there was no getting away.

The two teams stepped back away from the doors into the warehouse and took cover around the corners. Then one of the men in charge gave the signal, and a series of small explosions pounded the framing surrounding the door. The loud bangs shook the building's foundation and caused the ground under the intruders' feet to tremble.

"Go!" one man shouted.

Instantly, all of the armed cops, feds, and SWAT team members surged toward the door.

"The doors are blown," Anton said, knowing that his partner had seen the same thing. For a brief moment, their screens shifted and shuddered with static as the explosion rocked the building and sent a concussion blast through the warehouse.

For a second, Anton wondered if their aircraft would crash, but the machines stayed airborne. And as the dust and smoke rolled through the new openings in the walls, dark figures emerged through the clouds.

The invaders were carrying an assortment of weapons, mostly submachine guns and pistols, though a few bore shotguns.

"Take them out," Anton ordered.

The loud whine of the drones' motors filled the vacuous room and overpowered the ears of the intruders. The gunmen clutched at their ears and looked around in confusion, trying to figure out what was causing the deafening sound.

The first one to look up and discover the source was the first one taken down.

Gunter pressed a red button on the top of his radio controller, and the drone fired a small pellet at one of the men in the SWAT gear. The pellet struck him in the chest, just below the neck, and immediately the man began to gyrate, dropping to the ground as the charged projectile sent thousands of volts through the man's body.

The others saw him fall and immediately turned their heads upward to locate the source.

Anton and Gunter wasted no time.

Their thumbs rapidly pressed on the red buttons, emptying the reservoirs attached to the sides of their drones. The metal cylinders on each side puffed with a tiny cloud of air with each shot fired, driven by miniature CO_2 cartridges on the back of the aircraft.

Pellets pounded the intruders, dropping them like mosquitoes in bug spray. Within seconds, ten of the invading force were down on the ground, twitching and writhing in agony. After a minute, every single officer was incapacitated.

"Take out the rest," Anton ordered, satisfied that everyone in the building was out for the count.

He guided his aircraft through the new opening in the building and out into the open air. The sunlight momentarily blinded him, but he quickly recovered as the camera feed adjusted and he steered the drone around the perimeter until he located a collection of reinforcements.

They were mostly cops in uniform and were scrambling, confused by what was going on in the warehouse. They more than likely had heard the commotion—both with their ears and through the radios—and were trying to figure out if they should go in after the others or stay put as they were ordered.

Thanks to Anton and Gunter, they never had the chance.

The two Germans unleashed the remainder of their electrified projectiles at the cops, taking them down with ease.

Once they were sure the intruders were all out of commission,

Anton and his partner flew the machines back into the warehouse and landed them expertly in the office on top of the desk.

Anton removed his headset and placed it on the desk next to an open case. "Time to go," he said.

Gunter nodded and took off his goggles, setting them in the open case. He closed the radios and headset cases and carried one in each hand. Meanwhile, Anton walked quickly over to the computer closest to the door and clicked on a little icon in the top-right corner of the desktop screen. A window opened, and he clicked a button that read Confirm.

Then a countdown appeared on the screen. It only gave them two minutes to get out of the building, but that was more than enough time. Anton hit the button to open the secret passage again, and the two rapidly ascended the stairs. At the top, they scooped the drones off of the desk and carried them out the door.

They were already dressed in similar garb to the feds and cops who were still strewn about on the ground in the warehouse and outside in the parking lot. Once they were out of the office, they hurried across the building floor to where one of the units of cops was lying around, still writhing in pain.

Anton took one man's SWAT helmet and then kicked the guy in the head to knock him out. Gunter did the same, minus the kick, and then the two men hefted some of the police weapons and rushed out the door.

They found a squad car in the parking lot, unoccupied. The driver was lying on his side in the gravel, still rolling around from the voltage that had riddled his body. The keys were still in the ignition, and the motor was running.

"This one's as good as any," Anton said.

Gunter nodded and climbed into the driver's seat while Anton took up the passenger side.

The wheels spun, tires kicking gravel onto the cops as the men sped away from the scene, adding insult to injury.

By the time the fire in the subterranean room ignited, destroying all evidence of their presence, the two men were already a half mile away and gaining distance.

A pillar of black smoke rolled into the sky over the warehouse when they reached the outskirts of town. They heard firetrucks in the distance rushing to the scene, but the men who caused the blaze would never be found.

They would swap out the police car as soon as they reached a safe drop spot. For now, the local authorities and the feds had bigger issues.

The fire wouldn't consume the entire warehouse, and all of the men and women who took part in the assault would be evacuated unharmed, save for the guy with a lump on his skull.

Anton sighed and looked out the window, frustrated. "At least we know one thing is certain."

"What's that?" Gunter asked.

"They knew we were coming."

Gunter nodded. "What are we going to do next?"

Anton's breathing had returned to a normal, even rhythm. His heart no longer raced from exertion. "We find out who knew, who they told, and we eliminate them. If they have the stone, we steal it. If not, at least one threat will be gone."

13

ATLANTA

The three young visitors stared at Tara and Alex, eyes full of bewilderment and wonder. None of them knew what to say immediately—
until Corin finally found the obvious word they were all thinking.

"Quantium?" she asked. "What is quantium?"

"Ah," Alex said, raising a finger close to his shoulder, "that is the
million-dollar question. Actually, more like billion, with a b."

He turned to his computer and began typing. His fingers fluttered
across the keys like a butterfly going berserk. When he was done, he
hit the enter key, and the screen blinked. The new page that appeared
featured an article from an old newspaper.

The words Foo Fighters jumped out from the headline.

"Foo Fighters?" Diego asked. "Like the band? My mom loves them.
She's seen them a few times."

"I've seen them, too," Sam confessed. He'd been quiet for the last
several minutes, soaking in everything the others were saying.

"Yes. Well, no," Alex said. "What I mean is...the band's name
comes from a very real and very strange occurrence in history."

The kids exchanged confused looks.

"Seriously?" Desmond spoke first.

"Yep." Alex pointed at the article. "In World War II, Allied pilots reported seeing strange glowing orbs in the sky over their targets. They didn't know what these balls of light were or what could have caused them, but their instincts told them it was some kind of super secret Nazi technology. Initially, the pilots believed them to be weapons or even a special kind of fighter plane."

"Thus the name foo fighters," Tara added. "Although, we're not entirely sure why they chose the word *foo* other than it's the term the Air Force used to describe the UFOs they encountered during missions."

"Wait a second," Corin stopped them. "UFOs? What do you mean UFOs? Are you telling us that aliens are real and that the government has known about them all along?"

"I knew it," Diego whispered, almost to himself.

"Hold on, now," Alex said, putting his hands up in the air to calm down the hyperactive imaginations. "First of all, we're not saying it was aliens."

"You sound just like that guy on that aliens show on television, the one with the crazy hair. He always says he's not saying it's aliens, but it's aliens," Desmond countered.

"This is not really news, guys," Tara said in a matter-of-fact tone. "The government admitted to studying this stuff a few years ago. And now the military is opening up about their ongoing investigations into bizarre encounters and the belief that there is other life out there. That said," she went on before they could interrupt, "no, we're not dealing with aliens."

"There are other things at play here," Alex said. He clicked on a different tab, and a new image appeared on the screen. This one was a scene from a Hathor temple in Dendera.

"Ancient Egypt," Alex said then clicked again. "New Mexico and California." The next images were in the desert and showed strange orbs in the sky. Another was in Los Angeles. Alex clicked again and again, the same trend becoming apparent with every twitch of his finger. Each image that appeared on the computer monitor—some paintings dating back to hundreds or thousands of years ago—all depicted the same thing: glowing orbs in the sky.

"So," Corin said, "people have been spotting these orbs for thousands of years, all the way back to ancient Egypt?"

"Further back than that. Sumerian legends speak of them, as well. As do some of the ancient texts from Turkey and India. We believe there may be evidence of it in Australia, too, since the Aborigines are one of the earliest civilizations on Earth."

"Right. So, again, all these ancient cultures documented seeing these glowing orbs. What does that have to do with the theft from that museum and bracelet causing those lights to explode?"

"And that brings us back full circle," Tara said with a smile. "Quantium."

"Oh," Corin said with a nod, though she clearly didn't know what that meant.

"Quantium is an uncharted element, one that is so rare, most scientists don't believe it exists. Those who belong to the upper echelon of the science community are exceedingly skeptical about such things despite the fact that they've seen the theoretical models for it."

The blank looks on the kids' faces told Tara she'd gone a little too deep into the rabbit hole.

"Sorry, I forget you guys are in middle school. Basically, most scientists don't believe quantium is real even though quantum mechanics has essentially confirmed its existence. Up until now, it has been elusive. We think it might simply be extremely rare and difficult to find in the natural world."

"So, this is a naturally occurring element?" Corin asked. "Unlike some of the synthetic ones?"

"Correct," Alex confirmed with an obvious hint of surprise at her knowledge of the table of elements. "We suspect that throughout history, various peoples and cultures stumbled on to the element without knowing what it really was. They harnessed it by accident, creating strange and miraculous sights and wonders that wowed the people and further served their purpose of control. Often, these objects were used in religious ceremonies to prove that the priests or the people in charge were connected directly to the gods themselves."

The wheels were turning in the kids' minds, and Diego's was running at 100 miles per hour.

"You said 'by accident.' What did you mean by that?" he asked.

Tara took this one. "Relics, usually in the form of stones or crystals. For thousands of years, people have believed that certain kinds of stones and especially crystals possess almost magical powers. That's why so many amulets, medallions, and other kinds of protective jewelry were made for millennia. Of course, most of that stuff didn't have anything powerful to it. There were, however, a few items that were created that just happened to have traces of quantium in them. When those artifacts produced miraculous occurrences, like the one you saw in the video, people began trying to replicate the objects with minerals and crystals they believed were the same."

"But they weren't," Desmond said, catching up quickly. "They were just ordinary rocks and crystals."

"Exactly, but that didn't stop charlatans from selling those things to everyone who would buy them."

"So," Corin interrupted, "that necklace from the video, it had quantium in it? Why did that happen to the lights in the corner?"

"Great question," Alex said. "We're still in the early stages of learning about this strange element, but we think that Hitler's scientists were the closest to understanding its true power. His scientists were on the cutting edge of quantum physics. He had a deep interest in the bizarre and unexplainable side of science. He established a base in Poland where strange experiments were conducted. When the Allies took back Poland, they discovered this research facility and found it empty. Totally empty." He emphasized. "Even the most important weapons factories left traces of some of the things they were working on. Not this place. Everything was gone, like it had just vanished. The first troops to discover the place found a circular arrangement of concrete pillars. Each pillar had a metal loop attached to it as if chains had once been running through them to hold something. What that something was, we may never know, but there are rumors that Hitler was working on a device that could bend the layers of dimensions. It's even been rumored he was searching for a way to travel through time."

"Time travel?" Sam scoffed. "Seriously?"

When Alex and Tara's expressions remained unchanged, he could see they were serious.

"Really?" Sam demeanor changed instantly. "That's interesting. Did he succeed?"

"We don't think so," Alex said. "If he had, odds are the outcome of the war would have been much different."

"Unless, of course, he did succeed and his test pilots either chose not to come back or couldn't find their way. Still, it's doubtful. Time travel defies all natural known laws. They didn't fully understand quantium. No one who knows of it now or in the past does. What we do know is that it has a strange effect on the world around us, everything that falls into the perception of our five senses. It changes the reality or at least affects it in a weird way. Those glowing orbs are a symptom of its presence, though we still don't know what they are or why they exist."

The room fell into a pensive silence. For nearly a minute, no one said a thing. The kids were astounded by what they just heard. Time travel? Bending dimensional walls? An element that no one had ever heard of that could perpetuate these things and possibly more miraculous occurrences? It all sounded like fantasy.

Alex and Tara could see their young guests were beyond confused by this unexpected revelation. They'd come to ask questions about the Dare Stone and ended up getting a lesson in quantum physics. It was almost more than they were ready for, though they were no ordinary middle schoolers. They'd taken the information better than most, and Tara and Alex hadn't watered it down much. Still, the doubt on their faces told the truth.

"I understand that most of this seems unbelievable, unscientific, and at the very least unlikely," Alex started again.

"Actually," Corin said, "everything you're saying makes total sense."

Now it was the hosts' turn to look surprised. "What?" they said together.

"We've all heard of this kind of thing—not the quantium part, but we've read a little of the non-mathy stuff in regard to the quantum universe. It's pretty fascinating. And that side of science fills in gaps where traditional science can't."

"Yeah...that's true," Tara said, feeling like she was walking into some kind of conversational trap.

"The question we all have," Diego spoke up, "is what does any of this have to do with the Dare Stone?"

Alex's head snapped, and he rotated it in a full circle to emphasize how idiotic he felt. "Yes, of course. We digressed. A lot."

He turned and walked over to the stone sitting on the table and pointed at it. "We found traces of quantium in the Dare Stone, from the sample we took. This room," he waved a hand around, "is magnetically insulated and wrapped by four feet of concrete walls. We've noticed no dangerous effects of the element here. So, don't worry. The lights aren't going to blow out or anything."

"We think," Tara added.

"Right," Alex laughed uneasily.

"So, there were traces of this quantium stuff in the Chowan River Dare Stone?" Diego asked. "That's odd."

"We thought so, too. And believe us, we weren't borrowing it because of that. It was only in the last week we made this discovery from the micro sample."

"We first noticed the anomaly four days ago," Tara said. "We weren't sure what it was, and so we started running tests, doing more research, digging deep into both history and scientific study to see what we could find. It wasn't until we discovered a series of obscure papers from a former Nazi scientist that we learned about quantium and its mysterious power. That scientist, by the way, helped out with the Manhattan Project just a few hours north of here in Oak Ridge, Tennessee. You won't find him on any lists of accomplishments or commendations because after the war ended, he disappeared, and no one could find a trace of the guy."

"That's odd," Corin chirped.

"Yeah, no kidding. It seems everyone thought he went back to Germany to help rebuild, but there were no records indicating that."

Diego took a few wary steps toward the Dare Stone and stopped short of the table, bending forward at the hips to get a closer look at it.

"So, there you have it," Alex said. "Everything we know so far about this rock and its spooky abilities." He waved his hands around mimicking a ghost.

"Okay," Desmond said, "but what about the guys who were trying to steal this thing? Why did they want it, and why are they running around the planet trying to find this stuff? They must have some kind of plan for it."

"Oooh, like a super weapon," Corin said.

"The lights," Diego muttered, almost inaudibly.

"What?"

Corin and everyone else turned their attention to Diego. There was a reverent yet vague look on his drawn face.

"The foo fighters," he said. "That's it." He spun around and faced the others.

"What are you talking about, Bro?" Desmond asked. "You feeling okay? You look like you've seen a ghost."

Diego's lips twitched into a knowing grin. "Funny you should say that."

The other four scrunched their faces into bewildered frowns.

"Don't you see?" he asked, his voice now urgent and full of purpose. "The lights are the key." He looked to Tara and Alex. "You said that lights like that, like the ones the pilots reported from World War II, have been documented throughout history in various ways."

"Correct," Alex nodded, not sure where the kid was going with his train of thought.

"The Dare Stone's translation suggested that the natives in the area went crazy, something about angry spirits. It also says that some of the settlers may have gone mad, too."

"Right. What are you thinking?"

"Does quantium have any sort of effect on people's minds?"

Tara and Alex shared a look that contained no answers.

Tara shrugged. "We don't know. There's so little known about it that finding information is difficult at best. We're just beginning to scratch the surface of a surface that was just beginning to be scratched in the first place." The statement raised a few brows from the younger audience, but Sam stood tall with arms folded.

"Let's assume, for the moment, that it can affect the human mind. Like the drugs used in the MK Ultra program, except instead of using drugs that make people hallucinate, it was a sort of energy pattern."

Eyes around the room widened.

Diego found that he was surprising even himself at the revelation. He'd always been more into history and literature than math and science. Those were Corin's areas of expertise, but now he was diving in headfirst, and the answers looked plausible.

"So, you're saying that quantium might have been the cause of the disappearance of the settlers at Roanoke?" Alex asked, reaching the same conclusion as everyone else.

"It might be," Diego said. "In the text written on the stone, it says that there were angry spirits. Glowing orbs in the sky could easily be misconstrued as that. Even now, when people see those kinds of things, it spooks them. Take yourself back in time five hundred years, and imagine seeing that kind of stuff. The natural reaction would be to assume those glowing lights were some kind of spirits or ghosts. Mankind was extremely superstitious up until recently. Sure, some people still are, but back then superstitions were deeply rooted into the cultures and religions around the world. Like the thing with lightning and Thor's hammer or all those other things people didn't understand back then."

"That actually makes sense," Alex admitted. "The lights would be enough to creep out the settlers as well as the local native tribes. Especially the latter. It wouldn't be a stretch to think that the natives would consider the orbs to be a bad omen."

"Unless there was already quantium there," Tara countered. "In which case, the orbs would be a common occurrence."

"Which would mean an anomaly would have needed to happen, something that would make the glowing lights do something different that would give the appearance that they were unhappy."

"The establishment of the colony," Desmond said. "They viewed the newcomers as a threat."

"Some did; that much is for certain," Alex agreed. "You might be right. If some of the natives considered the settlers to be dangerous to their way of life, they would have taken action."

"Like attacking the colony," Tara realized. "That doesn't explain why the word *CROATOAN* was carved into a tree where the settlement had been."

"Actually," Diego protested, "It does."

14

ATLANTA

Everyone in the rooms locked their eyes on Diego as he explained.

"It's the perfect crime. Think about it." He put his hands out, pleading for the others to follow him down this crazy trail. "One group of natives freaks out about the newcomers. Then they see something off about their glowing orb thingies and decide that the colonists are a bad thing. So, they go on the warpath and take out most of the people in the settlement. The Dare Stone talks about a lot of fighting and death. Sounds like a battle happened there."

"And Eleanor Dare barely made it out alive," Corin added. "She escaped and wrote down what happened on that stone, including the strange details about the angry spirits, the natives, all of it. Then she disappeared as well. As far as we know, there were no survivors."

"Yep. And they pinned it on the Croatoan natives."

"The what now?" Alex asked. "I'm sorry; I'm a little behind on my history of the Lost Colony." He scratched the back of his head bashfully, and his cheeks reddened.

Diego passed him a forgiving smirk. " It's cool. I've just been interested in this topic for a while. See, during the search for the lost—

when the search parties were scouring the area near the coast for any sign of the settlers—the people in charge of the rescue operations found the word CROATOAN on a tree."

"That part I actually remember," Alex admitted.

"Right. Well, the Croatoans were a small island tribe off the coast of the Outer Banks. They inhabited a few small islands in the Atlantic, mostly kept to themselves, though not much else is known about them. They would have made the perfect scapegoat for an attack such as this one."

Tara and Alex stared in wide-eyed wonder at the boy as he talked about the investigation into the Lost Colony like he was a lauded college professor.

"When the search-and-rescue groups went to the islands," he continued, "they found no trace of the colonists and barely any natives, for that matter."

"I'm impressed," Tara confessed. "You know a lot about this...cold case."

Diego rolled his shoulders. "I like to read."

"So, all we have to do is invent a time machine, go back to the year the colonists disappeared, and we can stop the entire event from happening. Easy." Desmond snickered at his own joke. "Sounds like that's what the Germans were trying to do."

Corin offered a feeble smile but wasn't willing to part with a laugh at the attempt of humor.

"We don't need a time machine," Diego offered.

The group returned their attention to the boy. Diego swallowed hard at the attention and went on. "If there were some kind of orbs floating around in that area, it would stand to reason there would still be sightings in modern times, maybe even recently. Based on what you two told us about quantium, if there is a deposit of the stuff somewhere near the Outer Banks, then we should be able to find evidence of it. Surely, someone has reported seeing the strange lights in the sky since the colony at Roanoke disappeared almost five hundred years ago."

"A deposit of quantium?" Alex sounded dubious.

"He's right," Tara argued. "It wouldn't have to be much. You saw what that necklace did to the floodlights in that museum. And those beads on the necklace looked like they were nothing more than lava rock. Which means there wasn't much quantium in them, just like with this Dare Stone." She motioned to the rock on the table.

The kids looked over at the stone again.

The budding scientist in Corin couldn't keep her mouth shut. "I'm sorry, but have you two tested that thing out...you know, like on something electrical?"

"You mean like a couple of floodlights?" Alex said with a chuckle, seeing where she was going with the question.

Her cheeks turned pink. "Yeah, or something else. I dunno." She shrugged.

"No, we haven't had a chance yet, and honestly, we're a little scared to. We figure the only thing that's keeping us safe in this room is the magnetic insulation around it."

"When you brought it here from Brenau University, how was it transported? I assume in an insulated case?"

Tara nodded. "Yes. After what we saw at the museum in London, we knew that quantium resonates with electricity or devices that use electricity. We assume, up until then, that most of the work done with the stone was carried out with manual tools, the old-school way. Although there was a show a few years ago on the History Channel where a guy did a deeper dive with some high-tech equipment. It didn't seem to bother his gear."

"That does present a problem with the theory," Alex admitted.

Diego sighed and looked back to the computer. "Would you... would you mind running that footage from London again?"

"Sure. Why?"

"Just a hunch."

The group returned to the computer station and huddled around as Alex returned the screen to the video feed from the British Museum. They watched the heist again, and when the second thief extended the necklace toward the lights, Diego said, "Pause it there."

Alex did as he was told, freezing the figures on the screen in place.

Diego leaned closer and looked at something on the thief's arm. It was a metal band the color of brushed steel. The first time he saw the video, Diego didn't think anything of it. It was probably a watch or a bracelet, nothing of consequence, but now he wasn't so sure.

"Can you zoom in on his wrist?" Diego asked.

"Sure. Why?"

The answer became apparent when the image enlarged. The object on the man's wrist ballooned. It looked like nothing more than a watch wristband, except that there was no timepiece attached to it.

"What is that?" Diego asked, pointing to the band.

"Looks like a watch," Alex said. "Except there's no watch on it. Just a band."

"So, it's a men's bracelet," Tara offered.

"Maybe, but I don't see many men wearing bracelets like that," Alex countered. "Are you thinking that that bracelet triggered the quantium to interfere with the electrical current running to the lights?"

"Maybe," Diego said.

"That would make sense," Corin said quickly, jumping back into the conversation. "And it would explain why nothing happened when that guy doing the research on the television show didn't see anything strange happen."

"So, whatever that bracelet is made out of, it can harness the power of the quantium...or at least trigger it in some way," Tara realized in a solemn voice. "If they had enough of the element, and an army of people wearing those bracelets, they could knock out entire power grids."

"It probably wouldn't have to be an army," Alex added. "Just a few people in the right places could do some serious damage. And it goes beyond that. If they were strategic with their targets, they could wipe out huge databases of information stored on servers around the world. Anything not backed up on local devices could be wiped out. It could disrupt the world's currencies, trade, entire economies."

"That sounds bad," Sam said, chiming in for the first time in several minutes.

"Do you think that's what those thieves have in mind? Are they trying to gather as much quantium as they can so they can launch attacks like that?" Diego asked.

"We can't be certain, and we have no idea who they're working for. That's the other issue. Someone is pulling the strings, and I doubt it's those two from the video. We'll need to get back to figuring out where their next target will be."

"I thought you said the FBI was bringing them in," Desmond said.

"They are," Tara confirmed. "But those guys are probably just underlings working for someone else. As long as the head remains in place, they will just keep sending out new thugs to hit the next target, and the next, and so on until they have what they want."

Diego pondered the problem and turned away from the others to pace down to the end of the aisle and back. When he returned, he had a fierce look of determination in his eyes.

"We can't worry about that right now," Diego said. The others twisted their heads to look at him in surprise.

"What do you mean?" Desmond asked.

"I mean that dealing with the unknown is futile at the moment. Trying to figure out their next target; all of that stuff is great, but that's not why we're here, guys. We're here to solve the mystery of the Lost Colony."

"Yeah," Desmond agreed, "but there's a very real threat here. Who knows what these bad guys are up to? You heard Tara and Alex. They may have some kind of terrorist attack planned. Imagine if they succeeded. No internet. No YouTube or Netflix. No Amazon video. No Xbox online games. Is that the kind of world you want to live in?"

Sam snickered at the comment, but he knew the kid was right and that there were also much bigger things going on than what he listed.

"Don't you see?" Diego argued. "If those glowing orbs, the foo fighters, have anything to do with the disappearance of the Lost Colony, by solving that mystery we may be able to get to the bottom of what's going on with the two guys stealing artifacts."

Desmond inclined his head, realizing for the first time what his friend was getting at. "I see what you mean."

"It could work," Alex said, nodding. "But how do you propose we find out if your theory is right?"

Diego arched one eyebrow. "Have you ever heard of this little website called Google?"

15

ATLANTA

The group stood around the computer with Diego taking a seat in the chair. He worked quickly, typing faster than Tara or Alex thought possible for a kid his age. It didn't take him long to enter the keywords, and when he hit enter, the screen blinked and then brought the results for his query.

Everyone stood in stunned silence for a moment as they looked at the results page. There were links to multiple articles regarding his search term: glowing orbs in North Carolina.

There were several reports from across the state. More than one came from Charlotte, where people claimed to see glowing orbs in the sky a moment before the lights streaked away and disappeared into the darkness. Some of the links led to video footage of dancing orbs that floated in midair in a dark forest.

Diego clicked on that one first. The video began, and everyone leaned closer to see what would happen. It was hardly an action-packed thrill ride, but the footage did reveal what appeared to be floating balls of light, almost dangling in the darkness of the woods. Chills went up every spine in the room as they observed the phenomenon. Even Sam, who was usually as tough as they come, felt the hairs raise on the back of his neck.

"What is that?" Sam asked. He realized he sounded vulnerable and quickly changed his tone. "Looks weird, huh?"

No one seemed to hear him. They were so mesmerized by the sight that none could form the words to respond, even if they did hear him.

Diego clicked the back button and returned to the initial results of his search. He scrolled down beyond a few articles that related to the same topics about strange lights being seen in or near Charlotte. He stopped scrolling when he saw a link about a different topic. This one had to do with something called the Brown Mountain Lights.

"What's that one about?" Desmond asked, pointing at the same link that caught Diego's attention.

"Not sure but looks like something we should see."

A click of the mouse took the group to a page that immediately lost most credibility.

With the word _Ghosts_ at that top, Diego was tempted to completely forget about the site and go back to the search results for something a little less out there, but he started reading the first paragraph and decided to keep the computer on the page for a minute.

Each set of eyes scanned over the words, absorbing the information

Brown Mountain is a low ridge in Burke County, North Carolina. From what the website suggested, the mysterious glowing orbs had been observed for centuries, which was a surprise to Diego and the rest of his crew.

The Cherokee natives knew about them and saw them often. One of their beliefs was that the lights were the ghosts of Cherokee women searching for the souls of their fallen husbands who had died in battle, specifically a great battle that was fought between the Cherokee and the Catawba tribes.

One legend claimed that the orbs were residual energy from a search party that was looking for a murdered woman in the nineteenth century.

Perhaps the most intriguing of the stories was the one about two performers who sang a song about Brown Mountain.

Scott Wiseman and Myrtle Eleanor were musicians, often dubbed the "Sweethearts of Country Music" who toured the nation from the mid-1930s until around 1958. Their song about Brown Mountain seemed fairly innocuous at the time. As the group continued reading, however, the chills only grew more intense.

The song, written by Wiseman, depicts a story of a white man and a slave who go on a hunting trip into the mountains near Boone. According to the tale told in the lyrics, the two get lost, and eventually the slave returns to civilization without the other man. As the legend goes, the slave returned to the mountain every night with a lantern to search for his master, but he never found him. The song then goes on to say that the slave's quest continues from beyond the grave, and that that is the explanation behind the mysterious lights of Brown Mountain.

Wiseman, who was from the town of Boone, claimed he heard the oral tradition from his uncle, which was a common occurrence, especially in the Old South. Legends and folklore were often passed down from generation to generation by way of lyrics or simply through stories shared around campfires or at family reunions.

As he read the sentences, Sam recalled stories he'd heard from his grandfather that revolved around similar kinds of mysteries. Nothing haunted, but tales of hidden native and Civil War treasures abounded. Sam had taken in many such stories in his youth whenever his grandfather cornered him at a family gathering. Now, reading this particular legend brought all of those memories back around.

Apparently, Wiseman experienced a similar fate as a young man on hunting trips to Brown Mountain with his uncle. The song climbed to the top of the country music charts and, for a generation, offered the best-known theory regarding the lights, however unrealistic it may have been.

Many scientific explanations for the lights' existence emerged in the middle of the twentieth century.

One claim was that the glowing orbs were the result of headlights down in the valley somehow reflecting off of material or gas in the atmosphere. Some suggested that swamp gas was the culprit and the main cause of the strange phenomenon.

However, since the lights had been observed by countless witnesses for hundreds of years before automobiles were invented, that theory was easily discounted. Plus, the orbs were seen during 1916 when a flood shut down all traffic in the area, thus eliminating any possibility that car headlights were responsible for the occurrence.

As far as the swamp gas notion, there aren't any swamps in the area, so that theory had little to no validity.

There was one theory that did offer potential, though it was difficult to prove and, according to the article, had yet to be validated. This one suggested that the lights were a result of movement from the fault line under the mountain that produced some sort of magnetic or electrical resonance in the atmosphere above.

However, that hypothesis remained untested.

The group reached the end of the article, and the majority of them had more questions than answers. Before he clicked the back button again to return to the search results, Diego scrolled back up to the middle of the page and reread one of the paragraphs.

"This," he said, pointing at the lines of text. "This is our clue."

"What do you mean?" Corin asked. "How is any of that a clue? They're just stories and theories, Diego. There's nothing definitive there."

"I know that. I'm not saying there's anything concrete in this article. But don't you see?" He twisted his head and stared into her eyes with the intensity the midday sun. "The accounts from these stories; there is something in common with the Lost Colony."

"How so?" Tara asked first, though she knew everyone else was thinking the same thing.

"The disappearances," Diego said plainly. "Every one of these mysteries has to do with the disappearance of someone. The story about the guy who went missing in the song, the murder thing that might have actually been a missing-person issue, and let's not forget the Cherokee battle with the Catawba."

"It's a stretch," Alex admitted. "I don't mean to be Johnny Raincloud here. I'm just saying that while there does seem to be a common theme, it's loose. That's all."

"Loose is better than nothing," Corin argued.

"True."

"So," Desmond said, as if connecting all the dots for the first time, "your thought is that the Dare Stone, quantium, the Lost Colony, and all of these other stories, all of that relates somehow to these strange Brown Mountain orbs?"

"It's possible," Diego offered, doing his best to temper the excitement bubbling up inside him. He didn't think it was just a possibility. He believed it to be the answer they were looking for, the answer to a question that had been asked by so many over the last five centuries. Could it be that a middle school boy was the one to crack the code?

"Now that," Tara said with a grin, "is an impressive bit of sleuthing, young man."

"You think?" Diego tried not to sound too hopeful.

"Sure. I mean, it could be wrong, but as of right now, I'd say it's the best lead anyone's every had."

"The only thing we have left to do is go check out the lights for ourselves," Corin stated.

"What?" Diego turned to her. The rest followed suit, casting their gaze onto her.

"Why are you all looking at me like that?" She shrank back, folding under their stares like a lawn chair in a tornado.

"You're right," Diego said. "We need to go see these lights for ourselves."

"Now, hold on a second, guys," Alex said, raising his hands as if he were trying to stop traffic. "That's a big jump from coming up with an idea to actually driving several hours to go see something that may or may not exist. And even if it does, you're not guaranteed to get a show. That article clearly states that the lights appear when conditions are right, typically later in the summer or early fall when it's been dry."

"It hasn't rained in this region in a couple of weeks," Desmond countered. "Forest fire risk is pretty high right now."

"True," Alex said. "Still, how are you three going to get there? Tara and I would go with you, but we can't. As much as we'd like to go check out some mysterious happenings, we've got too much going on down here at the moment."

"I understand," Diego said with a solemn nod. He lowered his eyes to his lap for a moment. His pouting was cut short as Desmond spoke up.

"Sam?"

The muscular bodyguard started shaking his head before Desmond could even finish his name. The man knew exactly what the kid was thinking. Maybe not down to the details of the what, how, and when, but Sam definitely knew the kid was going to angle for him to drive them out to the countryside of North Carolina so they could investigate the bizarre glowing orbs for themselves.

"Oh no," Sam protested. "No way, guys. It's already afternoon now, and I'll have to get you home soon. We don't have time to drive up to...Charlotte or Boone or wherever it is you're wanting me to take you."

"We could go tomorrow?" Desmond offered.

"No, we can't. Remember? I have a date tomorrow night."

"Oh right." It was Desmond's turn to look dejected.

"Sorry, gang," Tara said. "I would really love to look deeper into this sort of stuff. Alex and I talk about it all the time. Our bosses, Sean and Tommy, they sometimes find artifacts that have odd qualities about them and seem to do miraculous things." She specifically thought about the high priest's breastplate that contained the Urim and the Thummim from the Old Testament of the Bible. She'd seen the black-and-white stones up close, even ran tests on the thing. She'd never been able to understand how it answered questions about the future so accurately.

Perhaps, at some point, Sean and Tommy would allow the two to start performing their own investigations into the unknown. For the time being, though, they were tied down to this lab, which was fine enough. They loved their laboratory and chose to spend most of their time there, even more than at their home, except on weekends.

"It's okay," Desmond said. Then his eyes lit up as an epiphany struck him. "Hey, Sam?"

"No."

"Just hear me out."

"No." Sam jerked his head and looked as though he might clamp his hands over his ears so he couldn't hear the request.

"What about a camping trip?"

"No."

"We could go up tonight, see the lights if they're there, and then come back first thing in the morning. You'll be home in plenty of time for your date, and it would give us a chance to get out of the house and do something. It's been so boring since we got back from Italy."

"Seriously? Boring? You guys should embrace boring, by the way. Boring is relaxing. When stuff gets fun or interesting, danger isn't typically far away."

"Come on, Sam. What's the big deal?" Desmond urged.

"The big deal? Really?" The man threw up his hands in exasperation. "The big deal is that we don't know if this is even real, first of all. Second, I have a date tomorrow night, and if I take you three camping, I know what's going to happen. I'll somehow get roped into one thing after another until it's past time for me to pick up my date, and then I'll miss out on it. Probably never get another chance."

"Wow," Diego said, solemnly. "Sounds like you really like this girl."

"I do!" Sam realized he snapped a little louder than intended. "I do," he softened his tone. "I really do. And I don't want to screw it up."

Corin put her arm around the big man and patted him on the middle of his back. "It's okay," she said in an attempt to offer him some comfort. "Sounds like you shouldn't miss out on that."

"Thank you," Sam said, resolute.

"And you're right. We do tend to get into mischief now and then."

His eyes narrowed with suspicion.

Meanwhile, Desmond and Diego looked absolutely astounded. Their plan was flying off the rails, and Corin was the one driving the engine.

"Exactly," Sam chirped, though this time there was a hint of doubt in his voice.

"We wouldn't want to cause you any trouble. We'll just go back to the house and hang out for the next few weeks until it's time to start school."

"Sounds like a plan." The dubious tone in his comment was impossible to ignore.

Corin turned to Tara and Alex. "Thank you, guys, so much for your time and for showing us all of this. I feel like we're backstage with a couple of rock stars."

Tara grinned from ear to ear, and Alex blushed as he beamed at her.

"Well, you three are welcome here anytime."

Sam coughed.

"Sorry, you four," Tara corrected.

Sam looked proud that he'd been included with the younger bunch.

"That's it?" Diego spat. "Seriously? We're just going to walk away from all this?"

"Yeah," Corin said. "We're just kids. What possible difference can we make? Besides, you could see from that video that the two people we're dealing with here are clearly better than Wayne and Carl. These people are pros. We wouldn't stand a chance against them."

Sam frowned but nodded curtly.

The look of dejection on Desmond's and Diego's faces cut through the room like a samurai blade. Their heads lowered, and the two boys relented with a pair of nods. Then, shoulders slumping, they started toward the exit.

"Where are you going?" Sam asked.

"Home," Desmond muttered. "We have no way to go see if those lights are real or if they have anything to do with the Lost Colony. So, what's the point of sticking around here? May as well go home and sit on the couch for the next couple of weeks."

Corin caught up with the two boys, and the three moped their way to the door. Sam stayed in place, contemplating more than he probably should have.

Finally, he let out an exasperated sigh and spun around. "Fine," he said.

The kids froze for a second, only daring to look at each other out of their peripheral vision.

Then Desmond spun around first. "Seriously?" he shouted.

"Under one condition," Sam said. "Actually, two conditions." He thought for a moment, wondering if there were more conditions he'd failed to account in his mind. "First, we have to be back by five p.m. tomorrow. No flex on that one. I am not—I repeat, not—missing my date."

"Understood," Corin said, turning slowly to meet his gaze like a professional poker player. "And two?"

"If we see those two from the video, you run. You understand. You scream, yell, holler, make as much noise as you can and get away. I don't want you three getting hurt. It was dangerous enough dealing with Carl and Wayne. These two are way more skilled than they were."

"Got it. See the bad guys, run away. Not a problem."

"Yeah," Diego agreed. "I've been running from bad guys all year, anyway."

Sam chuckled, not understanding the boy's meaning but going with it just the same. "Okay, then. We'll go home, you'll have thirty minutes to pack, and then we hit the road to head up to the mountains of North Carolina."

Cheers erupted from the kids. They jumped up and down and high-fived each other, overwhelmed by excitement.

"There's just one other thing," Sam said, cutting off their celebration.

The air sapped out of the room and the kids fell silent.

"What? You said two conditions. You thought of a third?" Desmond groused.

"No. Not a condition. It's just that you'll have to ask your parents first."

"That's not the only permission we have to ask for." He stared at Tara and Alex awkwardly. They exchanged confused glances, and then Desmond flicked his eyebrows up twice.

Tara and Alex shared a confused glanced before they looked back at the boy holding the stone.

16

WESTERN NORTH CAROLINA

Anton ended the call with their employer and slid the phone back into his pocket. He looked out over the valley below and ran a hand through his hair as he walked back to the car, parked a short distance away. He hadn't wanted Gunter to hear the conversation with their boss, knowing it could explode at any moment. Now that he thought about it, the man may actually have been able to cause the phone to explode—so extensive were his resources and abilities.

The conversation ended amicably enough, though it was clear the boss wasn't happy. Even so, he told Anton he trusted him and wanted him and Gunter to see it through.

Word about the heist had reached the order, as Anton knew it would. He had hoped he could delay his report on their progress for another day, but when the leadership called on their way out of Greenville he had no choice but to answer. Ignoring calls from their employers was explicitly prohibited.

With great reluctance, he'd answered and explained everything. The boss had been surprisingly understanding, as well as helpful.

It seemed their employer had a good idea as to who might have taken the stone and replaced it with a replica. While he was uncertain if the group who took it knew of their operations, he was inclined to believe they did—based purely on the nature of the IAA's body of work from the past.

The IAA was often involved in strange dealings in the esoteric realm of antiquities and rare artifacts. To Anton, it almost sounded as if the boss admired the IAA in some weird way.

Anton dismissed the notion and allowed his employer to continue the conversation, relaying the information he and Gunter would need to locate the real stone and secure it.

Then the conversation took a detour. The boss asked where Anton and Gunter were at that moment. Fear seeped into Anton's soul, even though he'd been trained not to feel fear from anyone or anything. This man was the one being on the planet that could cause that dread to creep back into him.

"I want you to go to North Carolina," he'd said.

Anton had initially been caught off guard by the order but allowed the man to explain.

"Go to the town of Boone. There you will find a mystery that has perplexed us for some time."

It sounded like he was taking Anton and Gunter off of their mission.

"What kind of mystery, sir?" Anton had asked.

"It's known as the Brown Mountain mystery—the Brown Mountain Lights, actually," the boss answered. "I will send you the coordinates for a place I would like you to inspect. This ties directly with the Dare Stone, and while it would be better if you had it in your possession, that won't be possible for the immediate future. The security at the IAA building is ahead of everything else in the world right now and with good reason. We won't be able to get in there without trying to blow up the building, and that would defeat the purpose. So, instead, we must be patient until the stone presents itself as an easier target."

"So, what is this mystery again, sir?"

"You'll know when you get there. It appears there may be a vein of quantium somewhere around Brown Mountain. Everywhere we've found the orbs, we've found the element. We must get to it before someone else does. I can already see that there have been a few internet searches regarding the element. So far, no one has found anything because I have expunged any information even closely related to quantium. Still, it's only a matter of time. Get to Boone immediately, and check in when you arrive. You shall have the coordinates within the next five minutes."

Anton recalled the end of the talk as he approached Gunter, who was sitting half on the edge of the hood with one leg draping down the quarter panel.

"What are we doing?" Gunter asked. He took a bite of a piece of bread and chewed. The two men had picked up a few crusty bread rolls and three or four pieces of cheese at a local farmer's market earlier. It was better than going into a supermarket or one of the large chain stores that happened to have a grocery section. Those places all had cameras, and the less Gunter and Anton were seen, the better.

"He wants us to go to a town called Boone. Shouldn't take too long to get there."

"What's in Boone?"

"A mountain."

Gunter's head cocked to one side like a curious puppy. "A mountain. What's so special about this mountain?"

"Lights," Anton said simply.

"Oh," Gunter didn't need further explanation. He sat for a moment in silence, pensive.

Anton could tell he wanted to say something else. "What?"

After a long inhale, Gunter looked out over the valley. "Did you tell him?"

"He knew. He didn't say that, but I could tell. He knew we didn't get the Dare Stone."

"And yet he's going to let us continue on the mission?" Gunter knew the price of failure. "It's not like him to be so forgiving."

Anton knew his partner was correct, but he didn't have an explanation. It certainly wasn't in their employer's nature to simply blow off a mission he regarded as so important. Unless...

"I wonder," Anton said, leaving the thought dangling in the mountain breeze. He sat on the edge of the hood opposite Gunter and looked out over the valley.

"Wonder what?"

A few more seconds drifted by before Anton answered. "Unless he knows that whoever took it will be coming our way."

"You mean toward this...Brown Mountain?"

"Yes," Anton confirmed with a nod.

"Why would he know that?"

For all his intelligence, Gunter had always been a linear thinker, incapable of thinking in layers or anticipating multiple moves ahead of where he was. It probably made him a bad chess player, though Anton had never played the game with him.

And it didn't surprise Anton that his partner didn't see the possibility of running up against the IAA. It was a stretch, at best. Even Anton knew that. Still, it was the only plausible explanation for why their boss—the man in charge of what was the most powerful secret organization on earth—hadn't reacted harshly to their failure.

"The two are connected," Anton said. "Brown Mountain and the Dare Stone; they must be related somehow."

"You mean, the stone is a device that is linked in a way to the mountains and the weird lights people claim to see?"

"Yes."

Gunter scrunched his forehead, his eyebrows tightening the gap over his nose to almost nothing. "Anton," he said, using the man's name for the first time in a while to emphasize his concern, "for that to be the case, Eleanor Dare would have had to know something was special about the stone. She would have had to visit the mountain and take it from that location. Are you saying that she specifically picked that stone to use for her message?"

"I know it sounds unlikely," Anton agreed partially. "But think about it. Why else would the boss be okay with letting it go if it wasn't the piece to a large puzzle?"

"So, let's say you're right, that this stone is a control or a key to something at Brown Mountain. What does it do?"

"Whatever is there in or on that mountain must react with the stone or the other way around. And I'm guessing whatever that substance is must be pretty powerful."

"Yeah, but what kind of power?" Gunter pressed.

"I don't know, but if it's the right kind, you could be talking about free energy. Since the dawn of electricity, the one who controls the power, holds the power;" Anton answered dryly.

"Did you just think of that?"

Anton shrugged and cocked his head. "Maybe."

The two of them had spent dozens of hours researching the bizarre disappearance of the colonists at Roanoke before breaking into the Brenau museum. They knew as much about the Roanoke colony as any layperson, and probably as much as many so-called experts. But some kind of secret source of ancient energy? They'd never heard anything remotely close to that. It would make sense why their employer wanted it, though, and if that was true, was there more of this strange element out there in the world?

Anton diverted the conversion back to the subject at hand. "So, let's walk ourselves back in time. Eleanor Dare is at the settlement, things get crazy, and a battle breaks out. She claims there are angry spirits haunting some of the men and many of the natives. We've already established we think those spirits are the lights, but what we don't know is what she did to try to stop it."

"You think she got away." Gunter inclined his head.

"Obviously, she got away," Anton said with a mild snicker. "She engraved the message of what happened on that stone. But why that stone? What if she went to the source of the angry spirits, the place where they were most prominent?"

"Well," Gunter shrugged, "she wouldn't have to escape to do that. She could have been taken prisoner by the natives and then escaped later."

"True. That's a good point. Or," he pondered the next idea for a moment, "more likely, she was off doing something, perhaps washing clothes or taking a walk, when the attack came."

"That would explain her temporary escape," Gunter admitted.

"And how nothing else happened to her. She must have seen the whole thing from a vantage point, a hiding spot." He could feel his pulse quickening. "So, she followed them. Trailed the natives back to Brown Mountain, where she waited, then took the stone."

"She'd have to have been a brave woman to do that, especially after seeing her child and husband..." He trailed off at the thought. Even hardened men like Gunter had a breaking point.

"Indeed," Anton agreed. "She must have had revenge on her mind, but when she got there, to the native settlement, instead of killing to get her payback, she took something valuable to them, something that they would miss desperately."

"The stone."

"The stone," Anton repeated with a nod. "Which is why the boss is okay with us screwing this one up, at least for now. He knows that whoever has the stone will likely trace its origin back to Brown Mountain."

"Where we will be waiting for them."

"Precisely."

17

WESTERN NORTH CAROLINA

Sam yawned as he held both hands on the steering wheel, tapping it incessantly as he tried to keep himself from drifting off to sleep. Normally, that wasn't a problem for him, but it had been a long day and an exceedingly exhausting drive from Atlanta to the forests of western North Carolina.

The sun hung far to the west, easing its way toward the horizon, though sunset wouldn't come for another hour or so.

Everyone needed a break to stretch and get some fresh air. The kids were getting irritated, though they'd held off asking the proverbial "Are we there yet?" since they knew it would only infuriate their driver. That didn't keep them from wondering when they were actually going to get to where they were heading, and Sam could tell their impatience was making them antsy.

As the vehicle began ascending the mountain, Sam was glad to have the sun at his back. He'd driven up mountain roads like this before when the sun was in his face. That made things difficult, even dangerous at times.

He recalled a childhood drive up to the top of Mount Washington in Vermont. Although he'd been young, the experience left a strong impression on him, an indent on his mind that he'd never forget. His dad had fought against the glare of the late afternoon sun as he rounded the precipitous curves on the drive up.

When they arrived at the top, he was greeted by fierce winds that were much colder than he could have imagined for that time of year. It was only later that he learned the top of that particular mountain boasted some of the most extreme temperature and weather changes on the planet.

He snapped his head to the side to refocus, realizing that daydreaming about the past was making him feel groggy.

"You okay up there?" Corin asked from the back.

Sam acted surprised and raised his eyebrows, glancing at her in the rearview mirror. "Who, me? Yeah, I'm good."

"You sure? You look a little tired."

He rolled his shoulders. "I am tired, but that's okay. This time tomorrow night we will be back in the ATL, and I'll be on a date with a beautiful woman. Doesn't get better than that."

Corin offered him an approving grin and returned her gaze out the window, where the rows of trees in the forest seemed to go on forever.

Sam no longer wore his usual suit and tie, the standard uniform that the kids had grown accustomed to. In fact, this was the first time Desmond could recall seeing the man in casual attire in years. The last instance was when they were in the Middle East on a hunt with Desmond's parents. It was the only time Desmond could recall seeing the man in shorts, and even then, his shirt was tucked in.

Now, though, Sam was dressed down, wearing a pair of khakis, a white T-shirt (untucked), and a baseball cap.

Desmond liked the look, as did his friends. Sam was wound too tight, or so they thought. That was one of the reasons they'd been surprised to learn he had a date with a real live woman. They didn't think the guy had the social aptitude to get a date.

Sam guided the black SUV around a long curve, and the vehicle began climbing again, this time up a steeper portion of the road.

Reading the kids' minds, he addressed their concerns before they could voice them. "We should be there soon, guys. I know it's been a while since we got out of the truck. I need to stretch, too." He hoped the promise of a break and the camaraderie of misery would alleviate their pains for just a few more minutes. In reality, it did little.

"There might be a pull-off up ahead. These kinds of places usually have stuff like that, national parks and such. If I spot one, we can get out and take a breather, maybe figure out where we want to go to see if we can locate those lights."

"Sounds good," Desmond said. He did appreciate Sam's effort in trying to make them feel better about the situation.

A few minutes of silence passed as the kids gazed with vapid eyes out the windows of the SUV. Sam scratched his head as a thought occurred to him.

"Hey, guys?" he said, cutting through the quiet cabin.

"Yeah?" Diego answered first.

"I was just thinking. The Lost Colony was in Roanoke."

"Uh, duuuuuh," Corin said, elongating the word to emphasize that the answer was obvious.

"Right. So, the coast of North Carolina is still hours away from here. You know that, right?"

It was a detail they'd actually not considered.

"My point," Sam went on, "is that's a long way from here. Your theory is that these mysterious lights on the mountain have something to do with the disappearance of the colony."

It was the first time they'd considered the problem, and it was a big one.

Diego furrowed his brow as he thought about the question. If the natives who attacked the colonists had come from this area, they would have had to make a long trek to reach the settlement on the coast. And how would they have known where the settlers were or how to find them? That was a question that potentially unraveled everything they'd thought of.

"The Dare Stone," Desmond said.

The others looked at him questioningly, including Sam through the mirror again.

"What about it?" Corin asked.

"It might be that Eleanor Dare, the woman who wrote on the stone, followed the tribes here."

"That would be a long way to go for a..." Sam caught himself.

"For a what?" Corin asked, sensing where he was going. "For a girl?"

He cleared his throat and tilted his head to the side, stretching his neck as if he was suddenly uncomfortable. "No," he corrected. "I was going to say woman, but a woman from an era where they wore uncomfortable clothes, usually heavy dresses and such. Plus, back then, women weren't encouraged to do physically strenuous activities like exercise or running or walking great distances."

"So, you're saying she couldn't do it because she was a girl?" Corin held back the grin that would have told him she had him pinned.

"No. You're right. There have been strong women throughout history, despite the oppression of men telling them what they can and can't do. Joan of Arc was one like that."

Corin let the grin out of its cage, and her lips creased wide.

Sam saw the expression and let out a sigh. "I'm just saying, it's a long journey for anyone. But I suppose if she was motivated enough, she might have done it. Still, that doesn't explain everything."

"Alex and Tara said the stone contained quantium," Diego chimed. "They also think that the same element may be what's causing these strange glowing orbs to hover in the sky over the mountain. If that's the case, the stone Eleanor Dare wrote her message on could be from this mountain. It might very well be something she stole from the natives to take back to the colony, perhaps as a token of payback or maybe because she hoped the orbs would guide potential rescuers to her location."

"That's a good theory," Desmond said to his friend. "Did you just come up with that?"

Diego jerked his head to the side. "No. I've been thinking about it for a while now. I knew that the colony was hours away from here by car, which meant on foot or on horse, it would probably be a couple of days' journey at minimum. So, I started wondering how she could have done it, why she would have done it, that sort of thing."

"Well, it seems to make sense."

"Thanks." Diego offered an appreciative smile.

The SUV rounded the next bend, and a view of the valleys and hills below came into their line of sight. As Sam predicted, a public overlook peeled off of the road to the right, offering panoramic vistas to visitors. There was only one car there with two men sitting on the hood. They appeared to be talking about something, but as Sam pulled off of the road and into the parking area, the men's heads turned and watched as the SUV drove by, easing into a spot in the middle of the lot.

Sam killed the engine and looked into the mirror. "Let's get out and stretch, huh? Take a breather for a few minutes?"

The kids agreed with nods as they eagerly opened their doors and exited the vehicle.

The air was still warm from the midsummer day, though it was cooler than down in the lower elevations. Even though Brown Mountain was situated in the Pisgah National Forest, its highest point was just over twenty-two hundred feet. Sam remembered that for every thousand feet in elevation, the temperature dropped around three degrees.

Sam put his hands up over his head and bound them together, then tilted his body one way then the other to stretch his back. Then he bent over at the hips and stretched his legs, reaching down to his toes and pressing his fingers into the asphalt.

"I'm impressed," Desmond said.

Sam straightened and looked quizzically at his young charge. "What?"

"I don't really think of strong guys like you as flexible. It's impressive you can stretch like that."

"Oh," Sam chuckled. "Flexibility is part of overall fitness, young one. Remember that." He pointed a finger at Desmond and then added a wink.

Desmond nodded and joined his friends at the rock wall that laid out the boundary of the overlook. It separated a precipice from a concrete sidewalk that wrapped around the parking area.

"It sure is pretty here," Corin said. She drew in a long breath and exhaled slowly, savoring the fresh mountain air.

"Yeah," her brother agreed. "It is." He was momentarily distracted by the two men who were sitting on their car. For a second, he thought they were looking at him, but when he turned to face them, he discovered they were busy chatting about something, though he couldn't hear what the two were saying.

Diego didn't think much of them and returned the group's conversation to the topic of the mysterious lights. "According to what I've read online, the lights don't appear until after dark, so we have a couple of hours to kill. I suggest we try to figure out where we want to set up camp for the night, then work out how we're going to watch for the orbs."

"I'm extremely curious if the Dare Stone is going to have any impact on the lights," Corin confessed. "Assuming, of course, that the lights appear at all."

"Right," Sam said. "Good commentary. Keep your expectations low, kids. These glowing orbs don't appear every night. I'd say it's a rare occurrence, based on what I heard you three saying and what I looked up online while you were packing your gear. We may well not see anything. So, don't get too disappointed." He sounded way too cheerful with his message of gloom.

"True," Desmond hedged, "but there's also a chance that we will see them tonight. And if our theory is correct about the stone, maybe that will improve the odds a little."

Sam didn't seem to care. He shrugged his shoulders and then leaned over the railing to look out across the valley. "Quite the view," he said. "You three let me know when you're ready to get back in the old SUV there and we'll head up the mountain, see what we can find in terms of camping."

18

WESTERN NORTH CAROLINA

Anton did his best not to slip off of the sedan's hood as he overheard the conversation from the newcomers to the overlook. Had he heard correctly? Surely, he and Gunter weren't that lucky.

It blew his mind that the two of them had, mere moments before, been talking about the exact same issue with the distance from Roanoke to here. They'd even gone over the same theory, the escape of Eleanor Dare, the reason she would have followed the tribes over such a long distance, and how she might have gotten back. Plus, the kids even had a similar theory about the stone, though Anton and Gunter already knew what they were doing in that regard. They were well aware that the stone was most definitely connected to the glowing orbs of Brown Mountain.

Those three kids and their...nanny or whoever the man was were talking about the glowing orbs. Not only that; they mentioned the Dare Stone. Were they the ones who retrieved the real stone from the museum in Gainesville? They were just kids. How was that possible?

He didn't have time to process all of those questions. When he'd first heard mention of the lights, his head virtually snapped itself off his neck. Then when the Dare Stone came up, he had to do a double take.

Anton eased himself off of the car's hood as he watched the SUV drive away, merging back onto the mountain road before he sprang into action.

"Did you hear that?" he asked his partner.

"Only bits and pieces, but I heard enough," Gunter confessed. "You think they really have it?"

"There's only one way to find out."

The two men climbed into the car, still not believing their luck.

Gunter turned the key, and the engine revved to life. He shifted quickly into reverse, stepped on the gas, and whipped the car around, deftly shifting back into gear to save time. The wheels spun, and the tires kicked loose bits of gravel and dust behind the sedan in its wake as the driver sped away toward the road and their quarry.

The sedan shot out onto the road without the driver thinking twice about looking for oncoming traffic. Why would he? Since they'd been there at the overlook, he hadn't seen a single vehicle go by. That was nearly thirty minutes without any sign of traffic, except for the SUV with the three kids and their babysitter.

So, it was only natural that at the exact moment Gunter stomped on the gas and launched their ride back onto the road that a faded red pickup truck would be barreling up the mountain.

The driver of the pickup jerked his steering wheel to the left to avoid the collision. Gunter didn't see the truck until it was too late. His instincts were to hit the brakes and turn away from the accident, but his effort only half succeeded. The two vehicles glanced off of each other, Anton's door smashing into the passenger side of the truck. The force of the crash jarred Gunter's hands off of the wheel for a moment and sent the sedan careening across the road and smashing headfirst into the rocks just beyond the shoulder.

The front of their car crumpled on impact. The airbags deployed instantly, and the two men's faces smacked into the inflated cushions. The abrupt blow sent the pain shooting through the men's faces, particularly from their noses.

Steam and smoke immediately streamed from the hood of the car as the red pickup truck slowed to a stop on the edge of the road, his vehicle relatively unscathed.

Anton's head rolled to the side, and he winced, grabbing his nose to check for blood. There was none, but it still hurt as if he'd been socked in the face by a heavyweight boxer.

The two impacts in the accident disoriented him, and for a moment he wasn't sure exactly what happened. A high-pitched tin rang in his left ear. He turned his head back the other direction and saw Gunter moving slightly, his head twisting and turning in an attempt to gather his senses and his bearings.

He, too, was completely disoriented.

The crash hadn't been at high speed—at least, Gunther hadn't been speeding. He couldn't have been going more than 15 or 20 miles per hour when they accelerated out of the parking area.

But the truck had been approaching full speed, probably 40 miles per hour, if Anton had to guess, though his skills of assessment were way off at the moment.

He sniffled and noticed movement out of his right eye.

The driver of the truck was getting out.

Anton clenched his teeth and drew the pistol out of his holster as the man approached with hands in the air, an angry scowl on his gray-bearded face. The guy was wearing a red-and-black flannel shirt with faded blue jeans and suspenders with the American flag on them. His trucker hat featured what Anton assumed to be the man's favorite beer on the logo, one that Anton knew to be cheap and watered down. Perfect for this hillbilly's palate.

Anton reached for the door handle and tried to pull it, but the latch wouldn't engage. He pulled again and again, desperation growing as the truck's driver drew near. The man was unarmed, though Anton knew that was only for the moment. If the guy sensed danger, he would quickly return to his truck and pull out a firearm from what was likely a considerable stash of concealed weapons. Perhaps he didn't have any guns on him, but Anton thought that unlikely, especially considering the man's appearance and the

stickers on his truck that featured no less than four weapons manu-
facturers and an NRA decal.

"What in the Sam Hill are you two idiots doing?" the man
shouted. His accent was beyond Southern. It was something else,
almost a dialect all its own, from the hill country. Anton had never
heard anything like it—not in person, anyway—but it was clear
enough English that he understood. The man's body language and
tone also warned of the anger coursing through him.

Even through the disorientation brought on by the crash, Anton
could think clearly enough to wonder why the man was so upset. His
beat-up old truck didn't appear to be much worse for the wear, not
that anyone would notice. There were dents all over the driver's side
and a big one on the back where the man had been rear-ended at
some point. From all accounts, the irritated older guy was a magnet
for wrecks of all kinds.

The man was only ten feet away when Anton felt the latch
engage. He shoved the door open with a creak as metal caught on
metal. He pressed his foot against the base of the door to get a little
more leverage and felt the thing give way, swinging open suddenly
with such speed that the approaching man paused.

"You two idiots coulda got yourselves kilt," the guy said in his thick
accent.

"You, too," Anton said and raised his weapon. "We're going to need
your truck."

The man's face reddened further. He was already angry. Now the
guy was beyond furious.

"What did you just say? You better put that thing down, pretty
boy. You don't want to mess with the likes of me."

"You're right," Anton agreed. "I don't."

He fired the electrified pellet at the man's chest and hit him
squarely in the sternum. The old man dropped to the ground in an
instant, his body shaking and gyrating from the charge coursing
through him.

The truck's engine rumbled, sputtering white clouds of exhaust
from the rattling tailpipe.

Anton heard the driver's side door creaking as the metal panels rubbed against another part of the warped vehicle. He rushed around and pulled on the handle to help Gunter out and then grabbed the man by the arm.

Gunter looked woozy, and when his feet planted on the ground, he lost his balance for a moment. Twin streams of blood oozed out of his nose, likely from the impact with the airbag.

"You okay?" Anton asked.

Gunter nodded groggily. "I will be in a few minutes." He looked over at the truck and then the unconscious man on the ground. "I guess we're taking his truck, then?"

"Looks like it."

"I guess you should probably drive for now." He forced a cracked smile.

Anton chuckled "Yeah, I guess so."

"The driver dead?"

"No," Anton jerked his head to the side. "That's now how you and I operate, as much as possible, anyway."

"I know. I just wasn't sure."

"Come on," Anton said. "Let's get you in the truck and catch up to those kids."

19

WESTERN NORTH CAROLINA

Sam stood up and dusted off his hands. He looked at the tent with a satisfied expression and nodded to himself. Then he glanced over at the other three similar tents. The kids were already done and sitting in folding chairs they'd brought along.

The man scoffed. "How did you three get yours done before me?" He stepped toward them with a curious smirk on his face.

"Maybe we're just smart like that," Desmond offered with his own sly expression.

"I suppose you are," Sam said.

The bodyguard looked around the campsite. The tents were staked and ready for later when they would hit the sack. Sam was ready for that moment now. Exhaustion gripped him with clawed fingers and tried to pull him in, but he knew he couldn't rest yet. Just because the day had been tiring didn't mean they were done. He couldn't just sack up for the night. They had work to do, and there was no way the kids were going to let him out of it, especially not now. Although he'd have been mad at himself if they drove all this way to see the mysterious glowing lights and then never left the campground.

"Sam?" Diego interrupted his daydream. "You okay?"

"Yeah. Me? I'm good. Sorry. Just thinking." The man looked around one more time. The cooler was situated next to the fire pit. All of the food was hanging safely from high limbs near a folding table they'd also brought along.

There were few other campers in the area, and the ones that *were* there for the weekend stayed mostly out of sight. They were situated in some of the more remote camping spots the area provided. Sam could relate. They wanted to get away from the world, including other people. This wasn't a particularly busy weekend for camping since many people were on other kinds of vacations. Sam was glad for that. The last thing he needed was to deal with questions from curious campers who happened to be roaming through the campground.

"So," Sam said, "where do you guys think we should set up for the show?" He glanced off toward the west. He couldn't see the sun through the trees, but he knew it was getting low. The sky over the canopy above was already turning pale shades of blue and gray with streaks of orange creeping in to signal the coming of sunset. "Probably a good idea to get going. It'll be dark soon, and once that happens, we may miss the lights—if they're going to appear at all."

"Hey," Diego said, sounding hurt. "They're gonna show. Okay? Have a little faith."

"Yeah, Sam. Don't be such a downer."

The man put up his hands defensively. "Fine. Fine. Take it easy. I'm sure the lights are going to make an appearance."

He didn't sound believable, but the three kids accepted his surrender.

"I was doing a little searching for that information," Corin said. "It seems like that overlook we stopped before is one of the better places for viewing the lights."

"Okay," Sam said with a shrug. "So, we go back there."

"That's one possibility. The other is that we go to the nearest point to the lights. Based on the images I've seen and the documentation of where the lights appear most frequently, I think we may be able to find a closer spot to check out the show."

Sam arched his right eyebrow in suspicion. "You sure that's a good idea? I wouldn't want to spook the ghosts or spirits or whatever it was that haunted Eleanor Dare." He chuckled to himself at the joke.

"Hilarious," Desmond said with a slow turn of his head. "I'm with Corin. If we can get closer, let's do it."

Before Sam could protest their decision in favor of the ease of going to the overlook again, Corin spoke up. "Great. All we have to do," she said, pointing at a map in her lap, "is head here, to this point on the ridge. We can park fairly close from what I can tell. The walk should only take a few minutes, maybe ten at most. From there, we'll have a downhill look at the lights when they appear. That way, we may be able to find the source of what's causing them."

Sam wanted to say "If they appear," but he kept his mouth shut. He also considered telling her that people had probably been executing her plan for a hundred years without any success tracking down the source of the strange light show. He refrained from that as well, deciding to let the kids have their fun.

"Fine," he relented. "We'll go to the top of the ridge."

They left their gear and campsite behind and climbed back into the SUV. Sam started the engine and steered out of their parking spot.

The drive to the end of the road at the ridge top was, as Corin had predicted, a short one. Ten minutes after leaving the campground, they pulled off of the road where several railroad ties marked a parking area. A wooden sign in the center of the gravel pull-off designated this as a trailhead.

"That the trail we take?" Sam asked, disinterested. All he could think about was getting some sleep.

"Yep," Corin said, glancing down at the map to make sure.

Desmond looked over from the front passenger seat at the bodyguard. He slapped him on the shoulder. "Come on, Sam. Snap out of it. This is gonna be awesome."

"Yeah, sure."

Sam opened the door and crawled out of the seat. He stretched his arms to get the blood circulating and then jumped up and down a few times, shaking out his legs.

Desmond and the others walked around behind the SUV and opened the rear gate, then pulled out three black cases.

"What are you doing?" Sam asked, noticing the kids removing the hard-shell cases.

"Taking my drones," Desmond answered in a matter-of-fact tone. "We may need them."

"Why would you need your drones?" Sam made no attempt to hide his bewilderment.

"I dunno," Desmond admitted. "We might want to get an aerial video of the occurrence. Would be cool to see from above or from up close—in case we can't get close enough."

Sam rolled his eyes but gave in. "Fine, but I'm not carrying those for you guys if they're too heavy. We'll leave them on the trail and pick them up on the way back."

"Sweet."

Desmond handed a case to Corin and one to Diego then closed the rear door. The three walked over to the trailhead, where Sam was already standing. The bodyguard handed out headlamps for the three so they wouldn't have to carry flashlights or use phone lights.

"Here," he said, giving the last one Diego. "These will keep your hands free for...whatever you might need your hands free for." He realized how silly he sounded and turned to head down the trail. "After you," he motioned with one arm."

Diego didn't hesitate. He flipped on his light and started down the trail, casting the eerie LED beam onto the path ahead.

The sun dipped farther toward the horizon in the west, and the sky continued to darken. The beautiful shades of orange, pink, and purple faded into deeper hues, signaling the coming of night.

Sam gave one last look back over his shoulder at the SUV. He thought he heard something. Another vehicle? He listened hard for several seconds and then convinced himself he was just being paranoid, then continued down the trail after the kids, his eyes darting left and right to make sure no wild animals posed a threat.

He would relax the moment they got back to the campsite.

––––––––––

Anton eased the truck into the parking area, letting it glide in neutral with the motor cut off. The tires crunching on the gravel road would cause enough noise to potentially alert their targets. He didn't need a growling, old truck motor giving off their position entirely.

He stepped on the brake the second he felt the front tire hit the railroad tie and then shifted the truck into park.

"You okay to go?" Anton asked, looking over at Gunter in the passenger seat.

"Yeah, I'm good now. Just needed a minute to regain my bearings, but I'm fine."

"Looks like they headed down that trail."

"Going to get a closer look at the lights, you think?"

Anton nodded. "Probably. Come on. We don't want to let them get too far ahead of us."

The two men climbed out of the truck and made their way onto the trail after the three kids and their bodyguard. Soon, they would have a potentially massive source of quantium for their boss, along with the infamous Dare Stone.

20

WESTERN NORTH CAROLINA

The Adventure Guild waited along the edge of the trail less than a quarter mile down from the road. As night settled in, they grew nervous—with anticipation, excitement, and with anxiety.

Animal life of a wide variety claimed the Pisgah National Forest as home. At any given moment, there were likely thousands of species surrounding the kids and their chaperone. Most of those species were insects, sure, but there was more than enough animal life to go around beyond the usual squirrels, chipmunks, and birds.

Coyotes bayed in the distance, casting their haunting calls into the night as both warning and challenge to prey or foe. Somewhere in a far-off valley, a lone wolf answered, though from the sounds of it the animal was nowhere close to the pack of coyotes.

At one point, Desmond saw a red fox trotting along through the underbrush. The animal was no more than fifty feet away and locked eyes with the boy as if wondering what in the world he was doing here in the fox's domain.

A North Carolina barred owl hooted from one of the low branches nearby and caused the entire group to start. Although likely no taller than a foot and a half, its call was so loud, so rapid fire, it seemed to come from a much larger, much more dangerous nocturnal predator.

Everyone exhaled. Sam chuckled at himself for letting a bird spook him.

So far, none of the more dangerous wildlife seemed to be in the area, but everyone stayed close. Sam wasn't much of a tracker, but he'd studied the craft a little in his spare time and could recognize bear tracks along with some of the other more threatening animal life. Still, if a bear were to happen upon their position, he wasn't confident the .40-cal Springfield at his hip would be enough to fend it off.

"You guys have any idea when this is supposed to happen?" Sam asked, sounding both irritated and exhausted. "We've been sitting here forever."

"It's been ten minutes," Corin said dryly.

"Feels like ten hours."

"Whatever. Have an energy bar or something. You'll be fine."

The big bodyguard shrank back at the sassy tone in her response, but he couldn't help but laugh a little. "Fair enough, lady. No need to snap."

He reached into his backpack and pulled out one of the prescribed energy bars, peeled open the wrapper, and took a bite. As he was chewing, Corin cast him a wayward glance.

"I wasn't being literal," she said with a laugh.

"No," he said, still chewing the food, "I think you were right. It was you guys' idea not to eat before we came up here."

"We didn't have time," Diego argued. "Now can we quiet down and pay attention?"

Sam considered asking if their conversation would somehow halt the appearance of the lights, but he decided to just keep his mouth shut and let the kids have their fun. What harm could it do, after all?

Then he remembered the wildlife in the darkness around them. They were in the animals' domain now. So, there was plenty of harm that could come from their little expedition. He stiffened his spine and felt at his hip to make sure the pistol was still there, even though he could feel the weight of it dangling from his belt. It was an old habit he'd picked up long ago, and he found himself reaching down to touch the weapon frequently depending on his task.

The four fell into a calm silence as they fixed their eyes down the slope toward a gully between ridges. More animals joined in the cacophony of forest sounds inundating their ears. Bobwhites and chuck-wills'-widows popped off their punctuated mating calls from somewhere nearby, though locating the birds' exact position was difficult. They were shy by nature save for their animated songs. Actually spotting one of the nocturnal birds was rare for novice bird watchers.

There were still no sounds of bears or cougars nearby, which were the two biggest threats in Sam's mind. And as long as the wolf and the coyotes also remained far away, he wasn't concerned, though perpetually on alert.

Around the thirty-minute mark, the group started growing restless. The kids knew that this wasn't something they could rush or force to happen, but they were still kids, and their level of patience hadn't reached full maturity yet.

Desmond sighed and looked over at his friends. "Maybe we should turn our headlamps off."

"You think they're having some kind of negative effect?" Diego asked seriously.

"I honestly don't know, but it could be."

"No way," Sam said. "We keep the lights on."

Desmond chuckled. "Someone's scared of the dark."

Sam pressed his lips together, nearly biting the lower. "No. I'm not afraid of the dark. It's just that we don't know what is out here, and these lights might help keep away some of the more dangerous animals."

"Fine," Desmond said, still containing his laughter. "We'll keep the lights on for you."

Sam rolled his eyes, knowing he was defeated and without any possible way to win the argument.

Just as Desmond was turning around to look back down the mountainside, a pale yellow glow crept over the group.

Every pair of eyes widened as they stared down the hill at the incredible sight. Four glowing balls of light ascended from the darkness of the forest and hung in the middle of the air, fifteen feet over the top of the canopy.

The hearts inside every witness pounded harder. Their minds raced with words they couldn't put together to form sentences. Sam babbled something incoherent as he pointed down the slope to the astounding vision.

"They're real," Diego muttered just above a whisper. "They're really real."

He gazed with his companions down at the anomaly. The glowing orbs appeared to hover there for a minute. Then something even more bizarre happened. The balls of light began to move. Not in circles or in haphazard motions but direct and steady. And they were heading toward the four witnesses.

"Um, Diego?" Desmond said, concerned, "why are they coming toward us?"

Diego shook his head. He couldn't think, couldn't reason it all out. Then it hit him. He sloughed off his backpack and laid it on the ground next to him. He unzipped the pack and though jittery nerves and shaking fingers fumbled with the zipper.

"They're getting closer, Diego," Corin reminded him in a haunted voice.

"I know."

Finally, the zipper opened wide enough for Diego to retrieve the contents of the bag. He pulled out the Chowan River Dare Stone and held it aloft. He didn't fully know why he did that, but he felt like it was the right thing to do.

The lights continued to approach, drawing closer and closer until they were only forty feet away from the group.

Sam drew his pistol, though he wasn't sure what kind of effect bullets would have on ghostly glowing orbs. He held the weapon out but kept it low, almost at waist level as he stepped in front of the kids.

"Stay back, guys," he ordered.

"No, Sam, it's okay," Diego said, still holding out the stone toward the lights.

The orbs continued toward them until they stopped only ten feet away, hovering about the same distance over the ground.

"We brought this," Diego said. He felt silly talking to four floating lights, but he didn't know what else to do.

"We come in peace," Desmond said and immediately regretted it.

"Seriously?" Corin asked. "We come in peace?"

Desmond shrugged and put his hands out wide. "I don't know what to say to a bunch of glowing balls."

The balls started back in the direction they came, and Diego felt his heart sink a little. He hoped there was something else to discover, something that would help them solve the mystery of both the Brown Mountain Lights and the Lost Colony.

Then one of the lights stopped moving and hovered in the air while the other three continued on. It twitched in an almost human way, as if beckoning the visitors to follow.

"Is it me, or did that thing just kind of tell us to follow it?" Corin asked.

"I think it did," Diego said. "Come on."

He started to step down the trail, but Sam grabbed him on the shoulder. "Hold on, pal. Let's not rush into this. That motion could have meant anything."

He looked up at the hovering ball and saw it jerk from side to side, as if saying no.

"Really?" Sam said. He sighed and let go of Diego's shoulder. "Stay close, okay? Everyone stick together. We still don't know what these things are and why they're here."

"Or what they want." Desmond added cheerfully, paying no mind to the ominous words that came out of his mouth.

"Not helping, Dez," Sam groused.

The four carefully picked their way down the trail, dipping between and around bushes or limbs that blocked the path. In some places, smooth rocks jutted out of the ground.

The descent to the location where the lights first appeared was easy enough, though everyone knew that climbing back up the hill would be twice as difficult. When the glowing orbs finally halted, they hovered over a huge outcropping of boulders.

The largest of the massive rocks was easily twenty feet wide and forty feet high, and Sam was immediately grateful they'd stuck to the path. A fall from that height would be serious, especially out here in the middle of the woods with no help in sight. The largest piece of rock was joined by two others on either side and appeared to be part of the same stone, merely cracked and separated in two places. The gaps between the three were so narrow, not even the kids could slip through. Upon closer examination, the group realized that these weren't boulders but simply exposed sections of the mountain that had burst through the earth over time.

"I don't get it," Sam stated loudly. "What's so special about these big rocks?"

Then Diego spotted something strange at the base of the stones. Three tablets that looked much like the Dare Stones were fitted into the base of the rock in a line near the ground. An empty slot took up where the fourth should have been, and the group immediately realized what had happened.

"Eleanor Dare took this stone from here," Diego said.

"She must have known it was important or that there was some kind of significance to this place," Corin added.

"Yeah, but what?" Desmond wondered.

Diego stepped close to the wall and stopped until he was standing under the glowing orbs. He stared down at the Chowan River Stone and then diverted his gaze to the empty slot on the rock face. He looked up at the lights that seemed to be peering down at him, eternal eyeless spheres. Then he knelt and extended the stone toward the surface of the boulder.

"Are you sure you should do that?" Sam asked, halting him for a moment. Diego froze and looked back over his shoulder. "I mean, if that Dare woman took it, she had to have her reasons, right?"

"She was protecting it," Diego said, as if the answer popped into his head from nowhere.

Sam's eyebrows knitted together. "What? Protecting it? What was she protecting?"

"I don't know, but I think we'll all know in a second."

He turned back to the enormous rock and slid the stone into place in the empty slot. The glowing orbs brightened for a moment and then began to pulse in a steady rhythm. The cadence growing more and more pronounced with every passing second.

Then the four lights slowly cruised toward the center stone. The group watched with rapt attention as the orbs moved closer to the rock surface. Then, as one, the four balls of light touched the hard rock.

Suddenly, the facade looked like it was melting back into itself from the center out. The illusion peeled away to the far edges of the stone until it revealed a gigantic opening into the mountain.

No one's lips remained closed, no eyes narrowed, as every member of the group gazed with astounded wonder at the unexpected revelation.

"It's...it's a gateway of some kind," Diego realized out loud. He took a step forward, almost unconsciously.

"And that stone was a key," Desmond said.

Sam noticed the boy's movement and reached out his hand, clutching Diego on the shoulder. "Wait. We don't know what's in there. We can't just go waltzing into some strange cave, especially one that was concealed by some...secret camouflaged door."

The lights hovered in the air just beyond the threshold, as if waiting for the group to follow. The glow emanating from the orbs illuminated a massive corridor, hewn from the rock of the mountain. The floor, walls, and ceiling were perfectly smooth, as if bored through with laser precision. Over the entrance, a door frame occupied the edges of the opening. Strange glyphs carved into the columns and the header glowed a dim blue.

"What are those letters?" Corin asked.

Diego shook his head. "Some kind of ancient hieroglyphs but not like anything I've ever seen. They look almost—"

"Don't say alien," Desmond said.

Diego looked over at his friend and cocked his head to the side, indicating that's exactly what he was going to say.

"I mean...if the shoe fits."

Desmond shook his head.

The orbs remained in place, still waiting.

"Guys," Diego broke the few seconds of silence, "we have to go in there."

"No. No way," Sam protested. "We can't do that. Besides, how do we know the second we go in there that this magical rock facade that was here a minute ago won't reappear and lock us in for good? I don't know about you guys, but I'm pretty sure your parents wouldn't like it if we vanished in the mountains. And I have no intention of starving to death in a magical cave."

"It's going to be okay," Diego reassured him.

"How do you know that?"

"Call it a hunch, Sam." Diego turned to face the bodyguard. "We are standing on the cusp of answers to a mystery that is older than this country, maybe thousands of years old. We don't know how long these lights have been appearing, what they mean, how it all works. This is the discovery of a lifetime, Sam. It's worth the risk."

Diego started forward, and the man grabbed his shoulder again.

"Hold on," Sam said. He checked his magazine again out of habit, making sure all the rounds were still in the pistol. Satisfied, Sam sighed and stepped in front of the kids. "I'll go first."

Diego, Corin, and Desmond shared a grin behind the man's back as they followed him into the mysterious, luminous cave, leaving the darkness of the forest behind.

21

WESTERN NORTH CAROLINA

The orbs moved forward into the passage, leading the group deeper into the mountain.

The height and breadth of the corridor was astonishing. It was easily twenty feet tall and fifteen feet wide. Whoever had designed and built this ancient hallway was either exceedingly large, or they had moved something through it that required an immense amount of space.

One interesting thing that the group noticed was that the light radiating from the orbs didn't seem to be isolated to a particular corona. Instead, it was as if the presence of the glowing balls caused the entire tunnel to illuminate, leaving no place for shadows anywhere.

Corin even noticed the strange phenomenon as she followed close behind Sam with the two boys on either side.

"Do you guys see that?" she asked.

"See what?" Diego wondered.

"This place; it's completely lit up. There are no shadows anywhere even though there should be behind us since the lights are ahead of us. But there aren't any."

The boys glanced back at their shoes and realized she was right.

"Whoa," Desmond said. "That's so weird."

It was then he realized they were beyond view of the entrance to the underground passage. The tunnel had veered slightly off to the left, and then back to the right in a shallow snakelike pattern.

"No turning back now," he muttered.

"Why would we?" Diego asked. "This is incredible."

He ran his finger along a line of glyphs that stretched out the length of the corridor on both walls. The characters were full of geometric shapes, lines, and patterns, interspersed with occasional squiggly lines and dots.

The four continued another hundred feet until the passage opened up, the width and height expanding until the group was greeted by the most incredible sight they could have ever imagined.

The glowing orbs continued gliding out into the open space until their light filled the entire chamber.

"Unreal," Corin said as she and the others stopped at the edge of a drop-off that fell to a floor fifty feet down.

They found themselves gazing up at a chamber that stretched the length of a football field in every direction in the shape of a square. The ceiling loomed hundreds of feet up to where four images were carved into the surface. The figures appeared to be human—two men and two women—but they were dressed in clothing unlike anything the visitors had ever seen before. The robes were long and flowing, parted in the middle, and they were surrounded by animals, some recognizable, others completely foreign.

As the orbs made their way out into the center of the space, the pictures on the ceiling brightened and then took on a light of their own. Vibrant colors filled the scenes depicted on the surface, filling the carvings with bright greens, blues, yellows, and reds. Deeper colors mingled with the others, burgundy, navy blue, and auburn.

"What is that?" Sam asked, pointing out into the middle of the artificial cavern.

The kids followed his finger to the center of the room, where an enormous structure rose from the smooth floor. It mirrored the rest of the interior, carved clean with no jagged or rough spots to be found. The "building," if that's what it was, climbed five stories high. The steep stone roof rose to a point in the center and was layered by dark marble tiles on one side and bright white marble on the other. In the front, columns held up the portico over the entrance with two massive doors of glimmering gold. Four obelisks stood apart from the building at each corner, separated by twenty feet but connected by a line of gold a foot wide and set into the ground.

"Is...is that a temple?" Desmond asked rhetorically.

Diego and Corin nodded absently. They each drew their phones out, seeing as the whole room was already illuminated, and snapped a few pictures.

"Sure looks like it," Diego said.

"Yeah, but what kind of temple? I mean, who was it built for?"

"And who built it?" Desmond added.

The orbs lingered in midair over the temple, and the vaulted ceiling's relief continued to expand outward, filling in every inch of the stone surface with more colors, both dark and light, separated to one side and the other.

More scenes washed over the walls, displaying a vast sky on one side, filled with stars and the moon, along with the planets of the solar system that were represented in such great detail that you would swear they'd been photographed by a modern-day astronomer. The scene of outer space took up two walls and then merged into a dawn and dusk that gave way to daylight and a setting of mountains, the sun, and radiant forests of green.

The glowing balls gradually descended toward the entrance of the temple and stopped when they were positioned in front of the doors, again waiting on the visitors to come forward.

Sam glanced to his right and noticed a stone staircase cut out of the wall. It crisscrossed its way down to the floor and was wide enough to not present a safety risk as long as everyone was careful.

"I don't want to say it, but looks like that's our way down to the floor level," Sam muttered.

The kids followed his gaze, totally unaware of the steps leading to the bottom of the cavern. They'd been so focused on everything else they never realized the stairs were there.

"You want to lead the way?" Desmond asked the bodyguard.

"Sure. You guys stay close behind me."

"Now that sounds like a good plan," a new voice interrupted.

The four spun around, Sam whipping his gun up to waist level as he turned.

One of the men, a guy with short blond hair, was pointing a weapon at Diego. The other gunman kept his weapon trained on Sam.

The blond clicked his tongue and shook his head. "Now, now. No need for that. Drop the gun, please, and no one will get hurt."

Sam hesitated, still thinking he could get the drop on the men, but it was too risky. These two wouldn't hesitated to cut him down. After that, who knew what would happen to the kids?

He didn't recognize the strange weapons in the gunmen's hands, but he knew they were some kind of firearms. The pistols were more curved than normal handguns, though they still featured a barrel and muzzle, sights on the top, and a grip and trigger like any other gun.

"Okay," Sam relented with more than a hint of regret. "Just take it easy. Point those things away from the kids if you don't mind."

"As soon as your gun is on the ground," Blondie said.

Sam put up his left hand and slowly lowered the pistol to the ground. Once it was at his feet, he stood back up and kicked it casually toward the gunmen, knowing they would ask him to do that next. It seemed that was always protocol for a situation like this. First, you surrender your weapon, then you kick it to the enemy.

"Thank you," Blondie said. "Now, you three, what's in those cases?"

The kids trembled with fear. They'd been in a tight spot before just a few weeks ago, but this was different, far different than anything they'd experienced in their short lives.

"Don't worry," the brown-haired man said in his thick accent. "These guns aren't for killing." His words had a slight impact, causing the kids to relax visibly, though they were still on guard.

"They're just my drones," Desmond sneered.

"Put the cases on the ground, please."

Desmond hesitated, and the man encouraged him by brandishing the weapon. "I really don't want to use this on a child," the brown-haired guy said. "It may not be lethal, but I assure you, it's not pleasant. So, please, put the cases on the ground, or I'll start with your friend, the babysitter."

"He's not a babysitter," Corin raged.

"She's right. I'm really not."

"Shut up and put the cases on the ground, or I start shooting," Blondie said. He'd clearly had enough.

"Fine," Desmond said and set his case on the ground at his feet. He pushed it forward a few inches, though he had no intention of making it easy on these two.

Corin and Diego followed his lead, both placing their cases at their feet.

"Step back, please," Blondie ordered.

The three kids took two cautious steps backward and then stopped when they were next to Sam.

The brown-haired guy stepped forward and picked up the nearest case. He took one big step backward and then knelt down, flipped open the case, and inspected the interior.

He looked over his shoulder at Blondie and gave a curt nod. "Kid wasn't lying. They're just drones."

Blondie's brow furrowed. "Why would you bring drones to this place?"

"I was thinking we might want some aerial footage of the lights," Desmond explained with a shrug. "Turns out it was just a waste of time and energy bringing them."

The two men seemed to accept the answer and shoved the cases off to the side after closing the opened one.

"Okay, now that we've taken care of business, please, go ahead." Blondie motioned down the staircase.

Sam squinted at the men. "You want us to go down there?"

"You were going to anyway. Please, go ahead. We'll be right behind you. So, don't try anything stupid. Okay?"

Sam clenched his jaw. His nostrils flared, and his eyes burned with anger. He couldn't believe he'd been so stupid, so careless to let these two men simply follow them down the mountain and into this...whatever it was, cave, temple.

He sighed and turned, motioning for the kids to go ahead of him. If he couldn't protect him with his skills and with his weapon, he would do so with his body. It was the least he could do at the moment.

Diego took the lead and began descending the stairs, followed closely by his sister and then Desmond and Sam. The two gunmen tucked in close behind, keeping their weapons trained on the group in case any of them decided to make a break for it.

Once they were at the bottom, everyone realized how truly massive the temple was.

The impressive structure towered over them. The doors in the entrance, too, were enormous, much like the passage they'd just left.

"To the temple doors, please," Blondie said, wagging his gun again as if he needed to remind his prisoners that he was still holding it.

The kids and their bodyguard trudged toward the entrance. They scuffed their feet as they moved, clearly in no hurry to reach the destination with their new wardens right behind them.

They climbed the short steps to the landing and proceeded ahead to where the glowing orbs still loomed over the entrance. When the group was near the doors, the balls of light shifted and continued on into the doorway, passing through it like ghosts in a haunted mansion.

The second the four orbs were gone, the doors creaked open on great iron hinges holding them in place.

The golden portal was unlike anything any of the group had ever seen in their lives, and even Blondie and Brownie stood there in stunned silence as they gazed upon the shimmering doorway.

If they thought that was incredible, what lay beyond the threshold of the temple was even more impressive, and befuddling.

In the center of the great room: a glowing white pyramid, no larger than a human head, floating over the floor.

The four orbs split up and moved, each taking a position in a corner until all the corners were illuminated. The pyramid brightened and began to spin slowly in place as it hung there in midair.

"What is that?" Desmond asked.

Blondie smirked and looked down at him. "That, my young companion, is quantium."

"Quantium?" Sam asked. "That's all there is?"

Brownie chuckled. "What you see there is the largest single cache of quantium ever to be discovered in the known world. Most of what we've seen is a mere trace compared to this." He looked over at his partner. "Now I see why he wasn't mad."

"Shut it," Blondie snapped. "Let's get the pyramid and go. The longer we stick around, the better our chances of getting caught."

The other man nodded and stepped toward the pyramid. The glowing object continued spinning slowly in place.

Brownie stopped when he realized that the floor was different in the center of the room. The lines of gold stretched from the corners into the center to form a single tile that was around forty square feet.

The second his foot touched the golden square, the pyramid brightened. A grinding sound permeated the room from above, and every single eye shot skyward to see what was going on.

Overhead, the angled ceiling peeled away, revealing some kind of strange machine. There were gears and levers. A model of the solar system occupied part of it, the planets moving slowing around the sun in the center. Other stars took up space around the solar system, though they appeared to be fixed and were not identified by name. One particular constellation drew the attention of Corin as she gazed upward at the incredible sight.

"Orion," she said, pointing up at one of the more easily recognizable star clusters.

"Hey, quiet," Blondie said, though the intricately designed ceiling held him in unbroken awe, as well.

Sam watched the man closely, waiting for a chance to make a move, but just as quick as the man's distraction came, it vanished, and Blondie was back to keeping a close eye on his prisoners, as well as his partner.

Brownie hesitated for a moment as he stood mere feet away from the glowing pyramid. He swallowed hard, unsure what was going to happen. He knelt down and set his tactical bag next to him on the floor. He unzipped it and withdrew a cube-shaped case that was roughly the size of the pyramid. How had their boss known? The box they'd been given was nearly a perfect match. Gunter didn't know where the man got his information, but one thing was clear: He knew far more than he let on to anyone, including some of his most trusted assets. Gunter couldn't help but wonder what other secrets his employer was keeping from him.

WESTERN NORTH CAROLINA

Gunter flipped open the case and discovered a golden metal liner inside. Gold? He'd been carrying around a box of gold this whole time? It wasn't shaped like a pyramid, though that's what he'd expected. His boss, it seemed, didn't know *everything*. That, or the man simply didn't take the shape of the quantium into account.

He lifted the case and took a step toward the spinning pyramid, holding out the box with the bottom aligned with the pyramid.

It was nearly under the spinning object when Diego shouted. "No, wait! You don't know what that will do!"

Brownie looked around at the boy with furious curiosity in his eyes. "Keep him quiet," the man ordered.

"No, you don't understand," Diego challenged. "If you remove that thing, it could bring down this temple on top of us. Even the entire cave. You have to listen to me."

"Do it," Blondie ordered. "And you, I told you to be quiet. I don't want to shock you, boy, but I will do it if there are any more outbursts. Understood?"

Diego didn't say anything, which was enough for Anton.

Gunter hesitated then looked up to the ceiling, the boy's words suddenly striking a sliver of fear into the man's heart.

"What are you waiting for, Gunter. Do it!" Anton realized he'd shouted the man's name, but it was no consequence now. Soon, these kids and their sitter would no longer be an issue.

Gunter still didn't look sure, but he wasn't about to disobey an order. He reluctantly twisted back to face the pyramid and pushed the box under it again with the lid hanging open. He swallowed visibly and hesitated. A deep pulse throbbed through the temple as he raised the cube closer and closer to the pyramid's base. The moment the bottom of the cube touched the glowing object, a high-pitched ring shot through the temple. It pierced the ears of everyone inside.

The kids and Sam clutched their ears with their hands, no longer caring that they were being held at gunpoint.

Anton instinctively reached for his ears, too, though he could only partially cover one while still holding the gun.

Gunter grimaced in agony at the piercing sound. His ears screamed for mercy, but he didn't stop. He forced the lid up over the top of the pyramid, and the ringing abruptly stopped. And with it, so did the light.

The room fell into utter darkness, then dim beams flickered to life and cast four white circles onto the floor.

"Our headlamps," Desmond whispered.

During the descent, they hadn't shut off the headlamps but didn't realize it with the glowing orbs casting so much light wherever they went. Now, in the pitch black of the temple, theirs were the only lights illuminating anything.

There was no sign of Gunter, but Anton readily made himself known.

"Stay where you are," he commanded, seeing that the kids were shifting subtly, as if having the lights made them invisible. Quite the opposite. "Put your lamps on the floor, please,"

Diego, Corin, and Desmond exchanged shadowed glances.

Corin spoke first. "But if you take our headlamps, we won't be able to see our way out of here."

Sam heard what she said but didn't add anything. Under the shadow of his light, his eyes flickered at the girl's wit.

"That is a shame, I know, but who knows? Maybe you will get lucky and stumble your way out of here at some point. By then, of course, we will be gone."

"Of course," Diego spat.

"No hard feelings, kids," Gunter said, stepping out of the shadows to where his partner stood.

Gunter turned on his phone's light and held it out toward the kids and their bodyguard. "Not bad for children," he quipped.

Corin was especially offended, and took an angry step forward.

"Not now," Desmond said. "Another time." He kept his voice low so the natural acoustics in the temple wouldn't carry his voice.

She bit her lip and clenched her jaw. "Fine," she surrendered.

The three took off their headlamps and placed them on the floor. Sam was slower to oblige, but he did after a moment of trepidation.

"Kick them to us."

Again, the captives looked to each other for answers but only found more questions. They stepped up to the lamps and kicked them toward the gunmen. The devices skidded across the smooth floor and stopped short. Anton kept his weapon leveled as he bent down and scooped up all four lamps.

"You've been worthy adversaries," he said. "It's a shame you're on the wrong side. We could use smart children like you."

Anton offered a cynical flash of his teeth, and then he turned and stalked toward the door.

"We're not children!" Corin yelled.

The two German men said nothing as they continued through the opening. The moment they were out of sight, the only light Sam and the kids could see was the residual dancing of the headlamps and Gunter's phone as the men climbed the staircase and headed toward the trail.

"When?" Sam asked.

"As soon as there's no trace of their lights," Corin answered.

"What?" Diego wondered, turning his head toward the sound of his companions.

"She used a little misdirection," Sam whispered, aware that the sounds of their voice might still carry up to where the passage led out of the temple. "She led those two to believe that the only lights we had were the headlamps."

"But we have our phones."

"Those guys didn't think about that because of what your sister said. It was a clever move."

He couldn't see it, but she was beaming with pride.

"Guys, they're gone," Desmond said. His was the first phone light to come on. Then the others joined in. The temple seemed less beautiful, less hospitable than before. In every corner, where the glowing orbs had hovered, now there were only stone spheres resting atop pillars.

"We have to get that thing back in here," Diego said. "It belongs here, and we have no idea what those two just did by taking it."

"What do you mean?" Sam asked.

"The natives here were terrified of the settlers. They went crazy probably because they believed that the colonists were going to destroy that pyramid or try to steal it. Fear is the greatest motivator of evil deeds," Diego said, feeling like he'd read that somewhere before. "They must have destroyed the colony and all its people out of fear of losing that pyramid."

"And if they were that afraid of that happening," Desmond added, "they must have been terrified of what could happen if the thing were taken."

"Exactly."

"So, what are we going to do? We can't catch them, and even if we could, how could we take them down?"

Desmond's eyes lingered as he gazed at the ground for a moment, lost in thought. Then he snapped his head up, the expression on his face alight with whatever idea had just popped into his noggin.

"I know a way."

The kids sprinted to the door of the temple with Sam close

behind. When they reached the entrance, Diego was tempted to look back, but he had a feeling it wouldn't be the last time he saw this temple.

They paused for a second at the base of the steps leading into the structure and muted their lights with their hands. Up in the tunnel, there was no sign of the two men.

"Come on. We have to hurry," Diego urged.

The group didn't need further encouragement. They dashed across the courtyard to the stone staircase and began their ascent. By the time they reached the first turn, their legs were already starting to flicker with fire. At the second turn, their muscles burned and swelled.

Their speed slowed significantly as they made the last turn, and even Sam was breathing heavily, taking in the musty air in huge gasps.

At the top of the steps, they trudged forward toward the opening of the corridor. Desmond's eyes frantically darted to where he'd left his case. Relief washed over him as he spotted all three drone cases.

"Grab your cases." He rushed over and picked his up. "We probably can't get a signal in here, but we can out there. And my radios have range extenders. As long as we keep them within a few miles, we should okay. Max range for these things is close to four miles."

"That far?" Sam asked.

"Tell you all about it later. We gotta run."

The other two had already picked up their drone cases and were moving toward the tunnel.

Sam nodded in agreement and ushered Desmond forward as he trotted past the other two kids. "Let me take the lead—in case they're setting a trap or an ambush."

He knew the two thieves were likely in a hurry to get out of there, but it was certainly possible. If something was going to happen to anyone in this group, Sam knew it needed to be him. The paranoid moviegoer in him feared that—at any second—a giant stone ball would come rolling out of another tunnel and squash them, or perhaps they would have to dodge poisonous darts or ancient flame throwers.

None of that happened.

They rounded the last curve in the tunnel and could smell the warm mountain air wafting into the corridor.

Sam neared the exit and lowered his flashlight. He reached for his hip out of habit and was reminded that his pistol was no longer there. He bit his lower lip and then stepped out of the passage and back onto the mountain soil.

The kids were close behind and quickly skidded to a stop at the edge of the boulder on the left.

Desmond set his case down and set to work. He looked at the other two and urged them on. "Get your radios and goggles ready, guys."

"But, we're not as good as you at this," Corin protested.

"You learned some things I showed you. It'll be fine."

"How are we going to see at night?" Diego asked.

"I equipped cameras that have a night-vision mode," Desmond beamed proudly. "And before you ask how these toys are going to catch the bad guys, Sam, these things can do up to a hundred under the right conditions."

Sam's eyebrows lifted in surprise. "Really?"

"Yeah, but that won't matter if we let them get too far away. Suit up, Adventure Guild."

He pulled the goggles down over his forehead and flipped on the radio. He'd already switched on the aircraft and set it on a nearby rock. The other two followed suit.

"Let's go get 'em," Desmond said. He pulled the goggles down over his eyes. The other two glanced at each other with uncertainty, then did the same.

23

WESTERN NORTH CAROLINA

The screens in the kids' goggles blinked to life. The world before them was now bathed in the eerie green light of night vision.

"Oh, weird," Corin said. "I can see myself."

"Yeah, cool, isn't it?" Desmond said with a smile. "Okay, just like we practiced, guys. Ease them up off the ground."

Each of the kids nudged the throttles, and the dormant motors whirred to life. The propellers chopped through the air in a blur, filling the surrounding forest with the sound of buzzing like a thousand bees rushing from the hive to attack.

"This is awesome," Diego said with a wide grin on his face.

"Yep. Now, follow me. Take it slow at first."

Corin was trying to do as she was told, but her thumb slipped on the stick, and her drone shot into the air like a rocket, accompanied with a loud whizzing that faded as the machine climbed into the atmosphere.

"Whoa," she said. "Sorry." For a few seconds, the sudden ascent disoriented her as the machine flew into the sky. When she let off, though, the camera quickly adjusted, and she could see the surrounding mountains, forests, valleys, and beyond from a view she never imagined. "This...is...amazing, Dez!" she exclaimed.

"Yeah, take it easy. Sounds like you went up pretty high. You got it under control?"

Corin looked through the goggles and into the night. She turned the aircraft a couple of times to get her bearings. "Yep. I'm good. Then she noticed something on the left edge of the view screen. Two lights suddenly switched on in the darkness near the top of the ridge. They stood out against the black backdrop, which was fortunate since the night vision only provided limited detail.

"I think I have them," Corin stated with a bit of uncertainty.

"Okay, keep eyes on them," Desmond ordered. "Hover there if you need to. I'm coming up to where you are."

Desmond's drone whined, and the machine darted upward into the night sky. He was cautious to keep an eye out for Corin's aircraft as his climbed through the air.

"Come on, Diego," Desmond said. "Let's get 'em."

Diego launched his drone into the sky, though at a much slower ascent. He still didn't feel comfortable whipping the machine around with reckless abandon like his friend or sister.

"The truck is on the move," Corin said. "They're heading back toward the split in the road."

"They're not going back to the campground. We know that," Desmond said.

Sam watched with rapt awe as the three kids guided their drones with the radios. He wanted to say something, wanted to help, but he knew there wasn't much he could do at the moment. Now that the drones were airborne and out of sight with the naked eye—save for the blinking red and green lights on the aircraft—their surroundings fell silent once more. He decided to focus most of his attention on the forest, just in case there were any dangerous creatures lurking about.

Corin maneuvered her drone toward the road, throttling forward with care on the radio's stick. Even with her caution, the powerful aircraft lurched forward with a jump.

"These things have quite a punch," she said.

"Yeah, just remember: subtle movements. You don't have to do a lot to get them going." Desmond offered the advice with a monotone voice as he tried to remain focused on the task at hand. He spun his drone around and locked in on the two lights as they started moving back up the road. "Target acquired," he said, feeling cool about using the lingo.

"I see them, too," Diego said as his machine climbed above the forest canopy and hovered momentarily a few hundred feet above. "What's the plan? It's not like we have any weapons on these things to slow down the truck or shoot out the tires."

"The drones *are* the weapons," Desmond mused. "Go for the drivers. Try to block their view, get in their way, anything we can to slow them down or cause them to lose control."

"Okay," Corin said.

"Follow me." Desmond throttled his drone ahead, passing Corin's as it zipped through the sky toward the top of the mountain. She tucked in close behind with Diego's aircraft bringing up the rear.

The drones reached the parking area at the top of the trail and flew over the SUV, each banking left in single file to fly over the gravel road. As Desmond lined up his machine over the road, he caught a cloud of dust in his vision.

"Pull up a little," he said, easing the machine higher to clear the rolling dust coming off the road from the thieves' tires. "Got some dust here."

"Roger that," Corin said, feeling cool that she could use the lingo, too.

Sam's ears pricked up at something in the woods. Was he just hearing things? He spun around and looked into the darkness. Nothing.

He was about to relax slightly when he heard the sound again. It was clear this time, definitely not a part of his imagination. A twig had snapped. Then a slight rustling of leaves. He could have blown off the latter as a result of the breeze wafting over the mountain, but the twig? That wasn't a coincidence. He shined his phone light around in a circle, scanning the perimeter for danger. Then he saw it.

"Um, kids, I don't want to rush you, but you might want to hurry this up. We have a problem." Sam's voice trembled, but he was trying to keep calm.

"What kind of problem?" Desmond asked as he guided his aircraft down the road.

"Not sure yet, just...um, you know, the sooner we can get out of here, the better."

"Not helping," Diego said.

"Yeah, sorry. Just...do your thing. I got it." Sam didn't sound certain, and there was no way he could hide it. He sidestepped away from the three kids for a second and picked up one of their hard-shell cases, closing the lid so he could swing the thing like a weapon. Without his gun, it was the only thing he could find. His toe struck something hard on the ground, and he bent down to pick up a jagged rock, leaving the case as a backup. He spun around again, shining the light in every direction as he searched for the source of noise he'd heard a moment before. Unfortunately, he could see nothing unusual, and the deep silence that permeated the forest only unnerved him further.

"I have eyes on the truck," Desmond announced as the two tail-lights came into view. He guided his aircraft forward, easily catching up with the speeding truck. The vehicle could only do 40 or 50 mph at most on the gravel road due to the curves and the nature of the loose gravel. Keeping control of the truck would be tricky under those circumstances, and at night it would only be made worse.

"Time to make their escape a little more difficult," Desmond said with a mischievous grin.

The drone darted forward, easily passing the truck below. He expertly spun the machine around and locked his gaze on the two men in the truck, their green forms apparently still unaware they were being followed or watched.

"You see the men?" Diego asked.

"Yeah, I got 'em." He twisted his drone around to focus on the road ahead so he didn't fly into a tree.

Corin's drone caught up and was right behind the vehicle while Diego's lingered behind hers.

"Corin?" Desmond asked.

"Yep?"

"You think you can land your drone in the back of that pickup truck?"

Her face tightened with concern. "I don't know. Maybe. Land on a moving target? We haven't done anything like that before."

"I know, but you have to try. And when you do, let the drone hit the truck bed hard."

"Hard?"

"Don't worry. You won't break it. And if you do, that's okay. I have a plan."

"Okay. Say when."

"Diego?" Desmond turned his attention to his other friend. "I need you to take my spot. Fly in front of the truck. When I tell you to, I need you to dive down in front of it and fly a few feet ahead of their windshield as long as you can."

"That's a pretty precise maneuver, Dez. I...I'm not sure I can do it."

"You can. I know you can. Just believe in yourself. It's easy. Just dive down in front of the truck, and lead the way."

"I...I don't know, Dez. I'm not sure about this."

"Believe in yourself, Diego. You got this. You're the one who figured out most of this whole mystery. If you can unravel a puzzle that's been unsolved for hundreds of years, this is a walk in the park."

He appreciated his friend's confidence. Was he right? Could he do this?

Diego thought about all the times he'd failed in life, all the moments he'd been unable to complete a task because he didn't have enough faith in himself to see it through. Then he pushed all of those doubts aside. He had to do this. There was no other way.

Sam heard another rustle in the woods less than thirty feet away. He spun to his left, and his phone's light reflected off of two sinister-looking orbs hovering a few feet off the ground. A twist of the light revealed the creature's fur, and then Sam knew they were in trouble. It was a wolf.

"Guys? Just letting you know that...um, no pressure, but we need to get moving."

"One minute," Desmond said. "What's got you so spooked, anyway?"

"Oh, um, nothing. I just...don't want to hang around here in the middle of the woods longer than we have to. Maybe we should head back."

"No can do, boss. We have these guys right where we want them. This is our only chance. We don't stop them now; they get away."

Sam clenched his jaw, and his grip on the jagged rock tightened. The wolf's glowing eyes eased forward, his paws moving almost imperceptibly over the ground. There was no more waiting. Sam had to put himself between the wolf and the three kids. He took a wary step toward the creature and waited, making sure the kids were safely behind him.

The wolf surged forward with a growl, and Sam raised the rock over his shoulder. He waited until the last second as the beast charged toward him. Then he fired the rock forward and struck the animal squarely in the right eye. The wolf yelped and then bent its front knees, rubbing the eye immediately as if that would save it from going blind. Between the furry legs, Sam saw the gash he'd opened up on the predator's face where the eye had been. The animal whimpered.

Sam grinned proudly as the wolf slunk away. *That was easy*, he thought.

The kids were oblivious to the lupine threat Sam had just saved them all from, and he allowed himself a slight grin as he glanced over at the trio. But his pride quickly faded as he saw another pair of eyes appear behind the first wolf. Sam's chest sank. "Seriously? Another one?"

"What?" Desmond asked as he flew his drone into position to the left of the truck. The vehicle turned through a long curve, slowing down slightly before it reached the next straightaway.

"Nothing. Nothing. Just, you know, do your thing. And maybe hurry," Sam snapped.

"Okay," Desmond said to the others. "They're about to come out of that bend in the road. This is our best shot at stopping them. We miss them here, and they're gone for good. Ready, Corin?"

"Ready."

"You ready, Diego?"

Diego flew his drone ahead to the straight stretch of road and stopped his machine a thousand feet ahead of the oncoming vehicle. "Ready as I can be."

"Good. Hold your positions."

The three watched the truck as it exited the turn and sped up along the straightaway. Huge plumes of dust rolled up from the back tires and sent a cloud into the sky.

Sam took another step forward as the second wolf approached, this one less cautious as it rustled leaves and broke twigs with its heavy paws. The creature was larger than the first, and for a moment Sam wondered if he'd injured this one's child.

The wolf rushed forward. Sam took a step toward it, clutching a hard-shell case in his right hand. The beast leaped. Sam swung hard, and the end of the case crunched against the wolf's jaw.

The creature yelped loudly as it hit the ground and shook its dazed head.

"What was that?" Corin asked, suddenly distracted by the sound.

"Nothing," Sam said. "Just a cough. Sorry."

Then the wolf growled and charged again.

"What was that sound?" Diego asked, trying to stay focused on the scene in his goggles.

"Just clearing my throat," Sam said with a grunt as he jumped at the wolf. The beast ducked away from Sam's wild swing and snapped at the man's leg. Sam deftly dodged the attempted bite and brought around the case with a hard backhand to the other side of the animal's jaw. This time, the creature wobbled, clearly dazed by the blow.

Sam didn't wait for another chance. He whipped the case around one more time and smacked the wolf squarely on the nose.

Instantly, the beast retreated back toward the darkness of the forest, its vision blurred from the strike on its now-broken nose and throbbing jaws. Within seconds, the wolf was gone as it slunk into the endless rows of tree trunks.

"Okay, Corin," Desmond said. "We only get one shot at this."

"Thanks. No pressure," she joked.

"Don't worry about it. We're humanity's only hope," Diego quipped with a smirk.

Corin shook her head. "Ready when you are, boys."

"Wait for it," Desmond said. "One more second, and there's a wider patch in the road." He held on for another moment and then said, "Go. Do it now."

"On my way."

Corin's drone surged forward, diving with incredible speed toward the back of the truck. She lined up the truck bed in her sights as she flew the machine at the target rumbling down the road.

Everything blurred around her as the drone picked up speed. She focused her eyes on the truck bed and the back of the cab, aiming the drone right at it.

"You're sure you want me to do this, Dez?" she asked with only seconds to spare. "Because I'm going to hit it hard."

"Crash the thing," he ordered. "The harder, the better."

"Okay." She pressed the throttle all the way forward, and the drone whined even louder, closing in on the target as it bumped along the gravel road. "Almost there," she said.

The back of the truck grew large in her screen, and then, suddenly, her goggles filled with static as the aircraft smashed into the back of the truck cab.

"Status, Diego," Desmond said.

Diego's drone was still hovering above the road ahead of the truck.

"They slammed on the brakes and are looking in the back through the rear window."

"Good, hammer it."

"What?"

"Aim for the windshield. Hit it as hard as you can!"

"But—"

"Do it!"

Diego didn't want to wreck his friend's drone, but he knew he had to trust that Desmond had a good reason for it.

He pushed the throttle forward and aimed straight for the windshield, grimacing as the machine sailed at the oncoming vehicle. Diego couldn't see the men's faces inside the truck cab, but he imagined there was a look of panic and curiosity coming from both as the blinking red and green lights sped toward them.

The driver saw the aircraft at the last second and tried to maneuver, swerving to the right to miss it, but Diego anticipated the move and rolled the drone the same direction. The moment before the aircraft smashed into the windshield, Diego saw the expressions on the men's faces. It was a look of fear and confusion, and one that put a smile on Diego's face as the drone crashed into the glass. He didn't see the machine shatter the windshield, sending dozens of spiderwebs cracking from the center all the way to every corner.

Desmond, though, saw the result and acted immediately, knowing full well what the driver would do.

The truck slowed for a moment as the driver rolled down his window and stuck his head out the window to see more clearly. The damaged windshield made it nearly impossible to get any visibility.

Desmond cracked a smile, seeing half of Diego's drone sticking out of the glass, embedded firmly in the center of the windshield. He must have been doing over 90 on impact to punch it through the glass.

The pickup began moving again, slower this time but still fast enough to make a getaway.

Not if Desmond could help it.

The other two took off their goggles and watched their friend as he expertly maneuvered the sticks on his radio and plunged his drone down out of the sky like a falcon descending on its prey.

Up ahead, there was another bend in the road, and Desmond knew he would only get one shot at this. He narrowed his eyes, focusing on the target as he guided the aircraft at blinding speed.

He took a deep breath, watching through the camera's eye. The sounds of the air whooshing and the propellers buzzing filled his ears. He made out the driver and aimed straight for him. Then he pushed the throttle all the way until it stopped moving. The drone zipped through the air with incredible speed.

Mere seconds before impact, the driver happened to see the blinking lights soaring toward him and immediately started rolling up the manual window as fast as he could.

It didn't help him.

Desmond's drone struck the glass with devastating force, blowing through the glass and sending shards all throughout the truck's cab. Only paused by the impact, the drone crunched into the driver's jaw and knocked him out cold before flying flopping helplessly into the center of the seat.

Desmond's goggles were still on, miraculously, and he watched as the passenger scrambled to try to correct the truck that was now veering off the road with an unconscious driver.

A loud crash came from up on the ridge down the road, and Desmond's goggles finally turned to snow.

"Did you get them?" Corin asked, eagerly.

Desmond pulled his headgear down around his neck, letting them dangle for a moment. Then he allowed a grin to creep over his face. "Yep. I think we did it."

Sam was still breathing heavily from his fight with the wolf, and the kids noticed he was holding one of the cases.

"What's wrong with you?" Desmond asked.

"Oh me? Nothing. Just, you know, fighting off wolves to keep you guys safe."

"Wolves?"

"Yeah, right," Diego said. "Come on. Let's get up there and get that pyramid back to where it belongs."

24

The police and the park rangers found the wrecked truck less than half an hour after Sam called in the report. The two Germans were, as of yet, officially unknown since they weren't carrying any identification, but with the help of the kids and the name they'd heard, the cops were confident they would be able to get a positive ID quickly.

The old man who owned the truck was more than happy to confirm those two were the ones who stole his pickup at gunpoint, and since the thieves still had the weapons on them when they were discovered unconscious at the scene, it was easy enough to arrest them. But before the police could put the men in the back of two cars, three other SUVs showed up, all black GMC Yukons. A dark-haired woman stepped out. She immediately took command of the scene and ordered the two suspects to be stowed in the back of her vehicles.

The cops protested at first—until they saw her credentials.

The lead investigator looked befuddled after he inspected her identification. "I've never seen that level of security clearance before. What are you, FBI, CIA?"

"I'm...something else," she said.

"Yes, ma'am, Ms. Starks. You certainly are."

She rolled her eyes at the cop's incredulity but blew it off. She turned to two similarly dressed agents, all wearing black, and ordered them to put the detainees in the SUVs.

"Thank you for your help, Officer," she said with a smirk.

"What...what should we tell the chief?" the cop asked.

"Tell them the feds took the case," she said over her shoulder with barely a twist of the head as she stalked back to her SUV.

"Oh...okay." The man couldn't have been more confused. As the doors to the SUV closed and the vehicles rumbled away, the cop turned to one of the others. "Who is Emily Starks?"

The guy's shoulders raised and fell. "Don't know, but it seems like she's someone we don't want to mess with. I've never heard of the kind of clearance she has."

The cops would never know the real reason why the men were there or why three kids and a bald, muscular babysitter just happened show up before they arrived.

The kids removed the drones—what was left of them—from the scene and stowed them in the SUV. Some of the parts could be fixed or replaced later. The more important thing in the truck, though, was the stolen Quantium.

They found it in the truck, uncertain if they should handle it or not. The thing could, after all, be dangerous or even putting out some kind of radiation. Still, it didn't seem like the kind of mysterious object that they should let slip into the hands of the local authorities.

The cops were actually the second call the kids and Sam made. The first had been to Atlanta. Tara and Alex hightailed it up to North Carolina and arrived a half hour after the last of the cops left.

The kids looked exhausted when the two showed up. And Alex and Tara also had a guest with them.

Tommy Schultz, the founder of the International Archaeological Agency, climbed out of the black Toyota 4Runner and crossed his arms at the sight of the three tired kids and their fatigued bodyguard.

"It looks like you three have managed to get yourselves into trouble again," Tommy said.

Desmond shrugged. "Those guys were the ones who were in trouble," he said with a toothy grin.

Tommy shook his head and then ran a hand through his thick brown hair. "I gotta say, I hope someday you three will consider coming to work for me. If you weren't so young, I'd hire you right now."

"You still can," Corin pried.

Tommy snorted. "They have these things called child-labor laws, but don't worry: when you three finish college, if you want it, you have a job waiting for you at the IAA."

The three beamed at the offer.

"So, what are you going to do with that?" Sam asked, pointing at the case that contained the pyramid.

Tommy walked over to where the case sat on the back of the other SUV's bumper. He flipped open the lid and gazed at the glowing object for a moment, his eyes gleaming with amazement. He closed the lid and sighed.

"This belongs where you found it," he said. "As much as I'd like to take this back to the lab and study it, I don't think we can."

"Why not?" Diego asked.

"We don't know what it's capable of, first of all," Tara answered. "And we don't know what will happen if it's removed from this mountain for too long, especially from the temple you told us about on the phone."

"We're going to put it back where you found it," Alex offered. "You said there was some sort of high-tech camouflage covering the entrance?"

The kids nodded collectively.

"Then it should be safe for a few hundred more years or until we can figure out what to do with it." He winked at the insinuation.

"So, that's it? You're just going to leave it here and pretend none of this happened?" Corin sounded both disappointed and disbelieving.

"Oh no. Not quite," Tommy said. "You have done an incredible service tonight, both to humanity and to history. Now we can finally get some closure on a mystery that was nearly five hundred years old. We have one more piece to the puzzle of what happened to the Lost Colony of Roanoke. And that is all thanks to you three."

Sam cleared his throat.

"Er, to you four," Tommy corrected himself. "Not only that; I've decided it's time for the IAA to start investigating things like this more thoroughly."

"Things like this?" Desmond asked.

"The unexplainable, stuff that doesn't make sense based on current scientific and mathematical knowledge."

"You mean, like supernatural or paranormal occurrences?" Diego asked.

"Precisely. I've seen enough of this kind of bizarre stuff out there to warrant taking a deeper look. So, I'd like to introduce you to the newest arm of the IAA." He put out a hand and motioned to Alex and Tara. "Say hello to the Paranormal Archaeology Division."

Alex's and Tara's eyes widened at the announcement.

"What?" Tara asked. "Are you serious?"

"As I can be," Tommy said with a grin. He cocked his head to the side. "What do you say? You two been in the lab long enough? You ready to get out there and start doing some real field work?"

They weren't sure what to say. Alex managed an "Absolutely, boss."

Tara was still gasping with excitement as she nodded.

"Excellent. There are way too many strange things out there, and not all of them are innocuous. We need people—nongovernment professionals—investigating these occurrences and anomalies with a scientific eye and an objective viewpoint."

"The PAD," Desmond realized.

"The P-A-D," Tommy corrected, "although, PAD works, too." He chuckled, turning to the three young sleuths. "Maybe someday, you three will be working for that division."

Diego smirked and stiffened his spine. "We already have our own division, Mr. Schultz."

The others nodded.

"We're the Adventure Guild."

EPILOGUE

ATLANTA

Diego and Corin hurried home from the first day of school, eager to get their homework done before they went to Desmond's house. They had a new mystery to research. It was something they'd discovered while talking to their social studies teacher about the American Civil War.

They rounded the corner of the street and jogged ahead until they reached their driveway then slowed to a march. They trudged up the short hill and walked around the sidewalk to the front door.

There, on the steps at the base of the door, was a cardboard box. The two looked at each other and then down at the package. Both of their names were on it and the sender was listed as "International Archaeological Agency, Atlanta, Georgia."

"Something from Tommy?" Corin asked.

Diego rolled his shoulders. "I guess so. Why would he be sending us something?"

"I have no idea."

"Let's go in and open it."

They unlocked the front door and stepped inside, Diego taking a quick look outside to make sure there was no one following them. He'd been doing that a lot lately, paying more attention to his surroundings, to the people nearby, to sounds he heard in the dark. It was becoming habitual, and while it was annoying at some moments, he felt like it would keep him and his sister safe if he were more on alert. They'd already enough bad guys to know the threat was real.

The two stepped into the house and took the package to the kitchen, where they set it on the table. Their parents weren't home yet, but they would be within the next half hour.

Diego set his backpack on the table near the box and walked over to the kitchen counter, took a sharp knife out of a wooden holder, and returned.

He made quick work of the tape and then allowed Corin to peel back the flaps so they could see inside.

Within the container were two matching bags. They were dark green with brown straps and a leather highlight on the front. Two mesh pouches on either end were sewn into the bag for carrying water bottles, and a flap hung over the front of each bag, along with two straps and buckles for securing their contents.

"Whoa," Diego said, pulling out one of the bags. He set it on the table as Corin removed the second.

"Mr. Schultz made these for us?" Corin asked.

"I guess so."

The phone in Diego's pocket rang, and he pulled it out. Upon seeing it was Desmond, he tapped the green button and answered.

"Hey, did you guys get a package from the IAA with a bag in it?"

"Yeah, we each got one."

"These things are so cool!" Desmond exclaimed.

"For sure. That was really nice of Mr. Schultz," Corin said through the phone that was now on speaker.

"You guys hurry up and do your homework. Still coming over after dinner?"

"You bet, man. We'll be there. Now that we're official, it looks like we have work to do," Diego said with pride.

"Definitely. Okay, cool. I'll see you two in a bit."

Diego ended the call and slid the device back in his pocket. He and his sister admired the bags for another minute, checking out the inside. They were about to leave and go to their rooms to start working when they noticed a letter in the bottom of the box.

Corin retrieved it and read it out loud. "Dear Adventure Guild, thank you for your assistance. Again. I think it's time that we make your group official, so I wanted to give you these archaeology bags as a gift. Carry them with pride. And know that you are always welcome at the IAA. Sincerely, Tommy."

The brother and sister beamed at each other and nodded with pride.

"Come on, Sis. Let's get to work," he said, nudging her shoulder with a balled fist.

They left their bags on the table and hurried to the stairs.

The kitchen light shone on the black letters printed on the dark green bags:

AG, Established 2018.

OTHER ADVENTURE GUILD BOOKS

THANK YOU

We'd just like to take a second to thank you for reading this and the other books in the series. We've had a wonderful time creating these stories and hope you've enjoyed them as well.

Want more Adventure Guild in the future? Drop us a line on Facebook or via email.

You can reach out at Facebook.com/ErnestDempsey and on his website at ernestdempsey.net.

Thanks again for taking the time to read these stories. We truly appreciate it.

Ernest and Chandler

For my mom and dad. Thanks for letting me work with one of the greatest literary minds to ever put words to a page. Being able to learn from Ernie has been the spark that I'm certain will light my life. Someday I know I'll point back to this time with him as the catalyst for all my success. - Chandler

For Scott and Jennifer. Thanks for letting me manipulate...I mean work with your son. - Ern

ACKNOWLEDGMENTS

None of this would be possible without an incredible team around us.

Thanks to our editors, Jason Whited and Anne Storer for their tremendous guidance in the production process.

Last but not least, a huge thanks to Elena and Li Graphics in Athens, Greece for designing incredible covers for these books.

Made in the USA
Lexington, KY
28 November 2019